#10

Coaching the River Rats

THE MITCHELL BROTHERS SERIES

THE MITCHELL BROTHERS

D0168787

#10
Coaching the River Rats

THE MITCHELL BROTHERS SERIES

Brian McFarlane

Fenn Publishing Company Ltd.
Bolton, Canada

COACHING THE RIVER RATS
BOOK TEN IN THE MITCHELL BROTHERS SERIES
A Fenn Publishing Book / First Published in 2005

Fenn Publishing Company Ltd.
Bolton, Ontario, Canada

Distributed in Canada by H.B. Fenn and Company Ltd.
Bolton, Ontario, Canada, L7E 1W2
www.hbfenn.com

Library and Archives Canada Cataloguing in Publication

McFarlane, Brian, 1931-
    Coaching the River Rats / Brian McFarlane.

(The Mitchell Brothers series ; 10)
For ages 8-12.
ISBN 1-55168-302-4

        I. Title. II. Series.
PS8575.F37C62 2005   jC813'.54   C2005-904686-4

COACHING THE RIVER RATS

NOTE FROM THE AUTHOR

Once again, the Mitchell brothers—Max and Marty—find excitement and adventure on the hockey rinks of the North Country.

When the hot-tempered coach of a local peewee team explodes in anger, acts disgracefully and resigns, Max and Marty are persuaded to replace him as co-coaches of a team with no practice times—one that has yet to win a game.

They soon discover they must deal with a number of problems common to minor hockey: pushy parents, biased referees, undisciplined players and a rival coach who advocates rough play and intimidation.

They lose their practice rink to vandals, are threatened by thugs and get hauled into court to face charges of inappropriate behaviour behind the bench.

Despite their problems, they are cheered by the play of a rookie female goalie, Nicole Falzone, by the skills of the Stanowski twins, two boys they discover playing on a farmer's pond, by the manner in which the River Rats respond to their coaching methods and...well, that's enough of the plot to whet your appetite.

Incidentally, although her role in the story is fictional, Nicole Falzone is a real person. A nine-year-old student at Our Lady of Annunciation School in Newmarket, Ontario, Nicole captured first place in a Mitchell Brothers story-writing contest in 2005.

Now join the Mitchell brothers as they cope with the problems and experience the fun of coaching a team of peewees.

Brian McFarlanc

CHAPTER 1

CLOSE CALL ON THIN ICE

Marty Mitchell put down the book he was reading and got up to look out the kitchen window. "It snowed again last night," he said to his older brother Max, who was finishing up his breakfast of toast and scrambled eggs. "Not much—just a couple of inches."

Max didn't reply at first. He was busy pursing his lips and blowing across a cup of hot chocolate. Finally, he said, "It always snows in Indian River, Marty. Often before Christmas. We're in the North Country, remember?"

Max reached across the kitchen table and read the cover of Marty's book: *Poems to Brighten Your Day.* "You're reading poetry now?" he asked in surprise. "Since when?"

Marty chuckled. "Since Miss Fallis, the librarian, recommended it. She thinks everyone should be a reader. It's a fun book."

Max was 17, blond haired and blue eyed, a handsome youth and a star athlete. He'd never had much interest in poetry. He was two years older than Marty.

"Why not read me a couple of poems while I eat my toast?" Max suggested. "I'd read the sports pages, but Dad took the paper with him when he walked to work this morning. And Mom went with him."

Marty thumbed through the pages of the book. "Here's one that made me laugh," he said, clearing his throat.

One bright day in the middle of the night,
Two dead boys got up to fight.
Back to back they faced each other,
Then drew their swords and shot each other.
A deaf policeman heard the noise,
And almost killed the two dead boys.

Max laughed out loud. He almost dropped his toast into his hot chocolate. "Now that's funny," he said, wiping his mouth. "Who wrote that?"

"Let's see," Marty answered, delving back into the book. "It's by Anon. No first name."

Max laughed harder. "Anon? That's short for anonymous, Marty. It means nobody knows who wrote it."

Marty shrugged. "Here's another by the same guy," he said.

2

I saw a man upon the stair.
I saw a man who wasn't there.
He wasn't there again today.
I really wish he'd go away.

"Cute," Max said approvingly. "One more and then we've got to plan our day."

Don't worry if your grades are low
And your rewards are few.
Remember that the mighty oak
Was once a nut like you.

Max grinned. "Enough, already. What are we going to do today? It's a beautiful Saturday. I hope you're not planning to read poetry all day."

"Let's go skiing," Marty said, moving to the window again. "It's a perfect day for cross-country."

"Hey, good idea." Max rose from the table and looked out over his brother's shoulder. "We'll go somewhere we've never been before. Over toward Turtle Creek. I'll call Trudy Reeves—she'll want to go with us."

Marty rolled his eyes. "What's this 'us' business?" he snorted. "You mean she'll want to go with *you.* Trudy follows you around like a puppy dog."

Max sighed and patted his blond hair. "I can't help it if Trudy thinks I look like a movie star."

"Movie star?" Marty exclaimed. "The only movie

star you look like is Rin Tin Tin, the famous dog. Or maybe Mickey Mouse. Or Popeye."

"Now, now, Marty," Max said soothingly. "Don't be jealous. I was the first-born and got all the looks and all the brains. It's too bad there wasn't much left over for you."

"Listen to Mr. Perfect," Marty said. "I admit you have the face of a saint—a Saint Bernard. And you're the only genius I know of with an IQ of less than 50."

Marty scrambled away from the kitchen table—just in case. Max had been known to throw a headlock on him and make him cry "uncle" more than once. This time, Max chose to ignore the insults and got back to the topic.

"Turtle Creek is only about ten miles from Indian River," he said. "I'll call Dad at the *Review*. Maybe we can borrow his car. Then we can park wherever we want and ski as far as we want."

"Good idea," Marty agreed. "And we can look for a Christmas tree on our way back. I'll bring the axe. When we're done, we can stop for burgers and ice cream at Merry Mabel's. It's your turn to treat."

"Ice cream? In December?"

"Sure, why not? There's no *season* for ice cream. It's not like strawberries or pumpkins."

"Maybe Trudy will offer to treat," Max suggested.

"All the better," Marty said. "See, you're not as dumb as a post like everybody says. And if Trudy doesn't offer, I'll tease her about you until she does."

"So it's okay with you if Trudy comes along?"

"Of course, you bozo. She's not bad company—especially when she brings her allowance."

Marty had a sudden thought. "Hey! There's a weird family living on a farm just this side of Turtle Creek. The Stanowskis. Joe Stanowski is in my class at school. Never says boo. He's got twin brothers in grade school. They're 11 or 12 years old and not very sociable, either."

"How do you know all that?" Max asked.

"You claim to have all the brains," Marty responded with a laugh. "How come I have all the answers?"

"You do have a nose for news," Max admitted. "That's why you'll make a good reporter someday. You can work with Dad running the *Indian River Review*."

"Don't forget that I'm a great photographer, too."

Max shrugged. He thought about something Marty had just said. "It's too bad the Stanowski kids miss out on so much. They hardly talk to anyone, and they run straight home after school. How do you even know where they live?"

"Because I pay attention, that's why. And I still

say they're weird," Marty said, getting up to search through the closet for his ski jacket and pants. "Come on, let's get going. Phone Dad—ask him if we can take the car." He ran a hand through his reddish-brown hair, trying to remember something.

"The axe, Marty. The axe."

"Oh, yeah. You didn't have to remind me."

Max, Marty and Trudy had been on the trail for about 20 minutes and were breathing heavily. They had followed a cross-country ski trail made by others until Max called over his shoulder, "Let's go up that rise. We'll be able to see in all directions from the top." Max broke trail and all three skiers were perspiring when they reached the summit.

They stopped and caught their breath.

"Great view from here," said Trudy. "It's a perfect winter day, and not a cloud in sight. Looks like 1936 is going to give us another white Christmas."

Marty shaded his eyes with a ski mitt and pointed. "What's that down in the valley?" he asked. "Somebody's moving down there."

"Let's go see," Max suggested. "Looks like some kids playing hockey on a pond."

They skied down the hill through snow-covered evergreens until they were a few hundred feet away from a small frozen pond, then coasted to a stop.

"Look at those kids skate," said Marty. "Especially the two in the green jerseys. They look like twins. And that looks like a girl playing in goal."

"The boys must be twins," Trudy said. "Same size, same looks, same dark hair. And what fun they're having!"

"They're great little stickhandlers," said Marty. He winked at Trudy. "Better than you, Max."

Max gave his brother a look and saw the twinkle in his eye. "Yeah, sure," he said. "But they do handle the puck well. The other kids can't get it away from them."

They were about to push ahead to get a closer look at the action on the ice, when they were startled by a deep voice that came from somewhere behind them.

"What are you kids doing on my property? Get off my land!"

Startled, they turned to face a large man who'd come up behind them, moving silently on snowshoes. He had a black beard, was solidly built and wore a dirty brown parka. He was cradling a shotgun under one arm. The skiers were shocked to see that it was pointed in their direction.

"Move it!" the man said angrily. "Scat! Get out of here! You're trespassing. And you're scaring any rabbits that might be about."

Max tried to reason with the stranger. "We're

sorry. We didn't know this was private property. We'll go around the pond and be on our way."

"No, you won't," barked the man in the parka. "Turn around and go back the way you came—up the hill." He waved his shotgun at the three teenagers. "And do it now!"

"Sure. Anything you say," Max said softly. He didn't like the mean look on the stranger's face. Or his cold eyes. And the shotgun was frightening. He figured it wasn't a good idea to aggravate the man. "Come on, guys. Let's go back." He began to turn around.

Meanwhile, the hockey action on the ice had stopped. The players had gathered together, watching the confrontation on the hill, wondering what was happening. As a group, they skated toward the near end of the pond where the ice was darker.

Crack!

The sound of breaking ice startled everyone.

"Look out! Get back!" Marty shrieked at the hockey players. A few scampered back to thicker ice, but the twin boys didn't make it. They plunged into the frigid water of the pond. "Help! Help!" they screamed.

Max glared at the man with the shotgun and shouted, "You can shoot me, mister, but I'm going after those boys."

Max raced to the edge of the pond, Marty and

Trudy close on his heels. He unsnapped his skis and stepped gingerly out on the ice, testing it. Marty and Trudy did likewise. The bearded man with the shotgun, making slower progress, slogged through the snow on his snowshoes, which he hastily removed at the shore.

In the water, the boys were gasping and shrieking. "We're drowning!" they wailed. "Our clothes and skates are pulling us down!"

"Don't panic!" Max shouted, trying to heed his own advice. He slipped down onto his stomach and pushed his way gingerly toward the open water. "Swim toward me and take my ski!" he ordered, holding it out in front of him. Out of the corner of his eye, a few feet away, he saw Marty following his lead—on his stomach, pushing a ski toward the second victim.

The boys stopped screaming, but they were still very frightened. Even though they were near panic and were blubbering, they followed Max's orders. They flailed their arms and moved through chunks of ice until each grasped the tip of a ski.

"Easy, now," Max said to the twins. "Hang on tight while I edge my way backwards. My brother's going to do the same." Using their elbows, Max and Marty moved backwards. But neither one could generate enough strength to pull the boys from the water. Then each brother felt pressure on his ankles. They were getting help. The man with the shotgun had thrown it aside with his snow-shoes, and he tugged Max by the legs, while Trudy assisted Marty. The boys struggled over the lip of the hole, kicked their way out of the water and were dragged to the shore and safety.

Both boys were exhausted and crying. Their teeth were chattering and one of them retched and coughed up some pond water.

The big man in the parka muttered, "Thank you, lads. Thank God you were here."

He lifted the twins, one under each powerful arm, and strode rapidly across the ice where it was thick. His heavy boots slid awkwardly over the slippery surface. He plunged into the snow on the far side and started up a rise, following a path made earlier by the hockey players. He paused for a moment at the top, turned and shouted back, "Meet me at the house! Bring my shotgun and my snowshoes!" Then he was gone.

"Wow! That happened fast," said Trudy. "It's lucky we skied over this way. That man might have saved one boy, but not both of them."

"He couldn't have slid out on the ice like we did," Marty added. "He weighs too much."

The Mitchell brothers, bent over with their hands resting on their knees, took a few moments to catch their breath.

"We'd better talk to those other kids," Max said, looking up. "Say, where the heck are they?"

"They're gone," said Marty. "As soon as they saw the twins were okay, they took off. They were scared. You know what I think—I think someone told them they shouldn't be out here. Someone told them not to skate on this pond."

Trudy nodded. "I'll bet it was the mean old guy in the parka. He sure scared me."

"Well, that ends our skiing," Marty muttered. "Let's turn around and go home."

Max picked up the shotgun. "Not so fast, Marty. We've got to return this to its owner. You collect his snowshoes."

CHAPTER 2
THE STRANGER'S HOME

The three teenagers knocked on the door of the dilapidated farmhouse. They had found the frame building by following the tracks left by the stranger in the worn parka.

"Door's open," a muffled voice called out. "C'mon in."

"This place is creepy," Trudy whispered, clutching Max by the arm. "Let's go home."

But Max had already pushed the door open and stepped inside. Trudy and Marty followed.

"I'm in the bathroom," the muffled voice bellowed. "Be out in a minute."

"He's going to the bathroom?" Marty whispered. "But where are the kids who nearly drowned?"

"He's not *going* to the bathroom, he's *in* the bathroom," Max answered. "Can't you hear the water running? He's giving those kids a hot bath, I'll bet."

They looked around. The room they were standing in was far from neat and tidy. The sofa and chairs were old and well used and there was clutter—lots of clutter. A newspaper spread out on the kitchen table. Unwashed cups and dishes in the sink. Boots lying in a puddle of water inside the front door. But there was warmth. A fire crackled in the fireplace and radiated a welcome heat throughout the room.

Down the hall, the bathroom door flew open and the big man filled the frame. His parka was gone and his shirtsleeves, soaking wet, were rolled up. There were traces of soapsuds in his beard.

"He's wearing red suspenders," Marty whispered. "Like Uncle Jake's. Uncle Jake says you can always trust a man who wears red suspenders."

"You're dripping water on my clean floor," the man said. "I just mopped it this morning. Oh well, it don't matter. Floors are meant to be dripped on from time to time. Sit down, I want to talk to you."

Hesitantly, Max, Marty and Trudy sat, squeezed together on the old sofa.

The man slumped in a chair and faced them. "First, let me get your names."

"We're the Mitchell brothers—Max and Marty," Max replied. "And this is our friend Trudy—Trudy Reeves."

"You the junior hockey players? The sons of the newspaper man—the owner of the *Review*?"

"That's right, sir. And you may have heard of Trudy. She's a hockey player, too, on our junior team. And the best female harness driver around."

The man nodded. He recognized her name. "You're the girl that won the Hambletonian not long ago. With Wizard the Wonder Horse. Congratulations."

"That's me," Trudy said. "Thank you."

"Let me say again how grateful I am you saved my boys—Lance and Larry," the man said. "I can't thank you enough for that. They both might have drowned if you hadn't come along. I might have gone under, too, for I surely would have gone in after them. And I'm not much better than one of my pigs when it comes to swimming. I feel bad about how I barked at you. I'm real sorry I tried to run you off my farm. But there's a gang of thugs living here in Turtle Creek. A mouthy bunch led by the Slugg brothers. Caught them trespassing a few weeks ago. I'm sure they were about to steal some of my pumpkins."

"We were glad to help," Max replied. "I guess you know now we're not members of a gang. Anyway, we didn't mean to trespass. Are the boys going to be all right?"

"Yep. They'll be fine. A hot bath, some hot chocolate and a few minutes in front of the fireplace should make their teeth stop chattering. They'll warm up in a hurry."

Marty realized something. "You're Mr. Stanowski, aren't you?" he asked. "Silas Stanowski."

"I am. Sorry. I should have introduced myself.

14

How'd you know my name?"

"From the photo on the mantle. There's a family picture and Joe is in it. Joe goes to our school—Indian River High."

"Joe's not here right now. He went into Turtle Creek today to buy some groceries. He'll be back soon."

Max began to get up. "Well, we can't stay, Mr. Stanowski. We've got to get back to Indian River. And we've got to chop down a Christmas tree on the way."

"Wait!" Mr. Stanowski fumbled in his pocket, pulled out an old wallet and produced a rumpled ten-dollar bill.

"This is for saving my boys," he said. "I wish I had more of a reward to offer but I'm just a poor pig farmer. Things have been kinda tough around here since my poor wife died."

"Your wife died?" Marty said. "Joe has no mother? He never said anything..."

"No, Joe's not much with words. Neither am I. But yes, my wife died a year ago. Cancer. The twins are miserable without her. They haven't laughed in weeks."

That explains it, Marty thought. *Why Joe doesn't mix, why he heads home right after school. The twins, too. They're grieving, their hearts broken. And they feel they have to get home and help their dad. It must be terrible to lose a mother.*

"We're so sorry," Trudy stammered. "We didn't know..."

Silas Stanowski got up from his chair. "Before you go, I want you to meet the twins," he said. "Lance! Larry! Come out here," he called. "Thank the folks who fished you from that pond."

The bathroom door burst open and two red-haired bundles of energy pushed their way through. They were freshly scrubbed and were wearing their pyjamas. One pair had "Lance" written on the front, the other "Larry." *They look so identical,* Max thought, *that the only way to tell them apart is by reading their shirts.*

The boys stopped when they saw three teenagers staring at them.

"Don't be shy," their father said. "Shake hands with these folks."

The boys shook hands with the Mitchell brothers and Trudy. In unison they said, "Thanks for saving us from drowning."

Everyone laughed. "Do they always say the same thing at the same time?" Marty asked.

"Not always," said Mr. Stanowski. "But often enough."

"Are you all warmed up after your close call?" Trudy asked.

"Yes, ma'am." Once again, the twins replied in unison.

Trudy giggled, then leaned forward and whispered

in Larry's ear. "Is there any way to tell you apart if you're not wearing your names? Or is it a secret?"

Larry put his finger to his face and ran it along his left eyebrow. "That's how," he said. "It's not a secret."

Trudy noticed the long scar, which was barely visible.

"Lance hit me with a hockey stick last year," Larry explained solemnly. "He didn't mean to do it, but it left a mark."

"Speaking of hockey, I've got some bad news for you two," Mr. Stanowski said.

"Uh oh," the twins said warily. "What bad news?"

"No more hockey on the pond," Mr. Stanowski said, "I warned you about that soft spot on the ice—told you to stay well away from it until it froze solid. And you promised me you would. So there'll be no more pond hockey for two weeks."

"Two weeks!" cried Lance.

"That's an eternity!" wailed Larry.

The boys turned and fled down a hallway. A bedroom door slammed.

"I hate to do that," Mr. Stanowski murmured. "It's not easy raising them alone. Fact is, I'd love to have been out on the ice with them. Maybe then they wouldn't have fallen through. But I can't be everywhere. If their mother was still here..."

"Things would be a lot different," Max finished.

"They sure would," said Mr. Stanowski, his voice breaking when he spoke.

"You must be a good coach," Marty said. "Lance and Larry are excellent players. Better than most kids their age in Indian River."

"Thanks, Marty," the big man said. "I was a pro once—played a couple of seasons in the NHL. So I taught them well at an early age. But now I have to punish them. And taking away their hockey is the only thing that seems to register. I plowed the snow off that pond a few days ago. Maybe I'll plow it back on again. Nobody should skate on it until it's safe."

"Gee, I hope it's frozen solid soon," Marty said. "Winters wouldn't be any fun without outdoor hockey. Not for me, anyway."

Outside the front door, while Max, Marty and Trudy were strapping on their skis, Mr. Stanowski said, "Thanks again, kids. I love my boys and I shudder to think of what might have happened today. Now I owe you big time. If you ever need anything—I mean anything—just ask and I'll be there in a second. I promise."

"Thank you. But I can't think of anything we need—not right now," Max said cheerily.

"Except a Christmas tree," added Marty.

"By golly, I forgot. I've got a whole stand of evergreens in a lot just down the road. Right hand side. You can't miss 'em. Take one. Take a dozen. And have a merry Christmas."

"You too, Mr. Stanowski," Max called out. "Nice to meet you."

CHAPTER 3

THE WINLESS TURTLES

"Did you have a nice Christmas, Trudy?" Marty asked. Max and Marty had sidled into the seats next to her at the Indian River Arena.

"Sure did," she replied. "I got some new hockey equipment from my folks. And thank you, Max and Marty, for the box of chocolates. That was sweet of you."

"You may have noticed I sampled a few from the top row," Marty said. "Just to make sure they weren't old and stale. I figured you wouldn't mind."

"I didn't even notice," Trudy fibbed. She turned to Max. "I see you're wearing the scarf I knitted you. You like it?"

"I love it," Max said with a grin. He didn't often wear a scarf, and canary yellow wasn't his favourite colour—but he didn't mind wearing the scarf Trudy had made.

He glanced at her hands. "And the gloves I bought you—they fit okay?"

"They're just fine. At first I didn't think orange would go with my green jacket, but now I think it does." She held her hands high, moving her fingers around in the gloves. "Don't you, Marty?"

"Sure...whatever you say," Marty murmured. He had no interest in clothes or in trying to match colours. He was wearing a red baseball cap, a purple parka with a torn pocket, green pants and brown boots. His pants were stained with glue, spilled when he attempted to build a model airplane.

"Brrr! It's cold in here," Trudy Reeves complained. "Winter came early this year. This old rink has to be the coldest one in the North Country. Maybe in all of North America."

"You never complain about the cold when you play with our junior team," Marty said, crunching a potato chip between his teeth.

"Better get used to it, Trudy," Max suggested, "if you're going to come to games in this old barn."

Trudy and the boys were there to cheer for Trudy's nephew, Tim Robbins, a 12-year-old forward with the Turtles, a local peewee team. Trudy, Max and Marty were sitting shoulder to shoulder among the parents of the Turtles—just a couple of rows behind the team bench. Not far away, a similar group of parents and fans sat behind the Wildcats' bench. Shouts of encouragement for both teams echoed off the roof of the dilapidated Indian River Arena.

"I'm glad we came," Max said enthusiastically. "For once, the Turtles are in the game. Usually, they take a pounding. But tonight they're only behind by a goal. And Tim is playing great hockey. I think they'll pull this one out."

Max Mitchell knew his hockey. He was a star forward and team captain of the Indian River junior team. His brother Marty, younger and stockier, was a goalie with the same club. And Trudy, also an excellent forward, was the only female player in the league. It was Marty who had doubts about the Turtles' ability to win the game, despite his brother's optimism.

"They must be wearing turtle-skin skates," Marty said, deadpan. "It takes them an hour to get from one end of the ice to the other." He laughed at his own joke.

"Seriously, goaltending's a big problem for the Turtles," he stated. "Chubby Thomas gives up a soft goal or two every game. He's been lucky so far."

"I feel so sorry for the Turtles, and especially for Tim," Trudy said. "They haven't won a game all season. And now they're losing again. Tim says their coach, Mr. Wilson, is so frustrated he's ready to blow a fuse."

"I'm not a big fan of Whizzer Wilson," Marty said in a hushed voice. "He's a tough guy, a mean guy.

And he's always blowing a fuse. Scares the bejabbers out of his players."

"He scares everybody when he plays the game, too," Max said. "He's a real bully, and he loves to fight. He's about 35 now, the goon of the senior league."

Marty whispered, "I hope he isn't teaching the Turtles to play dirty like he does."

"I'm sure he is," Max said. "Look at that big kid he's got on defence. Twice now he's slammed an opponent into the boards—hitting from behind—and taken a penalty. A good coach would bench a player who plays so recklessly. Instead, Whizzer pats him on the back."

"That's Wally Wilson, Whizzer's nephew," Trudy said. "Tim says Wally's always bragging in the dressing room about how tough he is. Tim says Whizzer told him once to rip another kid's head off, a smaller kid named Ferguson on another team. Wally went after Ferguson and broke his wrist with a swing of his stick. Tim said it was sickening. But Whizzer praised his nephew, saying, 'That's the way to play the game.'"

There was a whistle, and the teams changed lines.

"Great shift, Tim!" Trudy hollered through cupped hands when she saw her nephew come to the bench. He waved a glove, then shook his head in frustration and slumped on the bench.

"Hey, Robbins," the coach yelled. "Pay attention! Quit waving at your fan club."

"There was no need for him to say that," Max said. "All young players like to look up at the crowd and see if mom and dad are watching. It's normal."

"Tim tries so hard and he's so discouraged," Trudy said.

"If it wasn't for Tim the score wouldn't even be close," was Marty's comment. "He's the best player on the ice."

While Tim was taking a well-earned rest, the Wildcats surged in over the blue line. From a scramble in front of the Turtles' goal, the puck squirted loose and lay in front of the goal crease. Chubby Thomas lumbered toward it and was about to pounce on it when a forward on the Wildcats lashed out with his stick and batted it toward the goal. At the same time he kneed Chubby in the head. Chubby lost his balance and tumbled backwards, head over heels. The puck lodged in his equipment and both puck and goalie landed in the net—over the goal line.

The red light flashed. The linesman zipped in and pulled the puck from between Chubby's pads. "Too bad, kid," he sympathized. "But it's another goal."

Wally Wilson turned and gave Chubby a look of disgust, then slammed his stick against the goal post.

But Chubby was injured. Dazed from the blow to his head, he climbed slowly to his feet and clung to a goal post for support. Tim and his mates rushed over, propped him up and guided him slowly to the team bench. Tim grabbed a water bottle and handed it to the groggy goalie.

Chubby received little sympathy from Coach Wilson.

"What's the matter, kid? You're not going to chicken out on me, are you?"

"My head hurts," Chubby murmured. "And I feel sick to my stomach. I don't think I can play anymore."

"That's bull," snapped the coach. "A small concussion maybe. A tiny one. Nothin' to worry about—it happens in hockey. You've had a rest. Now get back in there."

"But..."

"No buts! I said get back in there!" Wilson snarled, even as he patted Chubby on the back, feigning concern and support. He whispered in Chubby's ear, "Don't you dare pull this crap on me!"

Chubby was on the verge of tears, but he shrugged and skated back to his net. A few fans applauded his pluck.

"He shouldn't be playing," Trudy said, concerned. "They should have called a doctor."

Moments later, Chubby misplayed a shot that

rolled through his pads and stopped just short of the goal line. And he fell awkwardly when he left his net to clear a loose puck and missed it entirely.

Chubby was obviously not himself. And when he put a rebound right on the stick blade of an opposing forward, who promptly scored on him, some in the crowd began to jeer.

The Wildcats owned a 3–0 lead.

Max, Marty and Trudy let out a collective groan after the Wildcats' third goal. Then they sat up in surprise, attracted by a commotion at the Turtles' bench.

They were shocked to see Whizzer Wilson grab a stick—Tim's extra stick—and smash it against the boards in a show of disgust. He pushed the stick back in Tim's hands. Tim looked ruefully at the cracked blade.

"Yer playin' lousy," Whizzer bellowed. "Yer all lousy. All but Wally."

Max, Marty and Trudy heard him use stronger, more profane language as he shook his fist at the players on the ice.

Trudy was disturbed and left her seat. "I don't need to hear him talk to kids like that," she said, "I'm going to the ladies' room."

In the stands, others who'd come to support the Turtles followed the coach's lead. Their support wilted and they became almost as critical of the dejected Turtles.

"Inexcusable, boys! You've gotta help your goalie!" roared a man in a thick fur coat. "No wonder you're losing."

"The goalie stinks!" bellowed an angry parent. It was a cruel condemnation and it surprised the Mitchell brothers.

"If he's hurt, get him outta there!" another man roared.

Wildcat supporters joined in with taunts of their own.

"Hey, goalie! Time to quit."

"Think you could stop a basketball, kid?"

The crestfallen goalie, Chubby Thomas, heard the cruel remarks—how could he not?—and stood in his net with his head down, still woozy, not wanting to face his critics. He took off a glove and wiped a tear from his eye. Then he skated in a tight little circle and slammed his stick against the goal post.

Chubby's mother, who was sitting close to the Mitchells, hid her face in her hands. "I can't stand it," she murmured. "I feel so sorry for my boy. Hockey's supposed to be fun."

"It is fun—most of the time," Marty turned and said. "But not tonight."

"But we're accustomed to *playing* the game, being on the ice," Max reminded his brother. "It's a lot different watching from the stands. As players, we don't get to hear a lot of the stuff the parents say. It's depressing to sit up here and listen to all the criticism."

Shortly after play resumed, Tim Robbins leaped back on the ice, just in time to throw himself in front of an opposing player, a puck-carrier skating in fast with his head down.

Wham!

Tim's solid check knocked the Wildcat on his backside. "You rat!" gasped the forward.

Max pumped an arm and chuckled. "What a great check!" he said.

But the whistle blew. The referee, a young fellow in his late teens, waved Tim Robbins to the penalty box.

"What for?" Max heard himself shout. "It was a clean check. No penalty!"

"Robber!" screamed Marty. "Bad call, Ref!"

The referee ignored the complaints of Max and Marty and many of the fans. But he could hardly ignore the screams of outrage from the Turtles' coach. Whizzer Wilson went berserk. He berated the official with foul language and whacked the boards with Tim's hockey stick until it shattered. He hurled a couple of water bottles at the referee. One of them struck the official on the side of the head, and blood spurted from a deep cut. Whizzer found a spare stick and was about to hurl it like a spear, when suddenly the stick was yanked from his hands. Max had leaped from his seat and raced to the bench. He rushed up behind the coach and pulled the stick from his grasp. "That's enough!" he shouted. "You might hit a player, you fool! It's bad enough you hit the referee. Calm down."

Whizzer Wilson was even more enraged by Max's interference.

"Stay out of this, Mitchell. It's none of your business," he snarled. He thrust out both arms and pushed Max backwards into the first row of seats. Max struggled to his feet and would have gone after Wilson, but strong arms held him back.

"Take it easy, son." An elderly man clutched Max by his sleeve in a farmer's grip and cautioned him. "That coach is a madman. He's liable to whack you with a hockey stick."

By then the referee was at the Turtles' bench, venting his anger at the coach. "You're outta the game, Wilson." He raised his thumb. "Unsportsmanlike conduct. Get going!"

But Wilson's tirade wasn't over. As the referee turned and skated away, another burst of foul language spewed from Wilson's mouth. Then he spat on the ice.

Wilson's tantrum shocked the spectators. It prompted one father to remark, "That guy's an idiot. I don't want him coaching my kid."

Chubby Thomas' mother agreed. "That's the last game my son will play for the Turtles," she said, disgusted. "I'd rather have him in figure skating. Or ballet."

Marty hid his face. The thought of the rotund goalie in ballet or on figure skates cracked him up.

The young referee, still dizzy from the blow to his head and holding a towel to his wound, skated to the official's box. He picked up a microphone to announce: "Folks, this game is over. The actions of the Turtles' coach will not be tolerated—not by me anyway. You all saw what happened. I'm quitting. And when my head clears I may decide to take legal action against Coach Wilson. So I'm awarding the game to the Wildcats."

He skated off to a mixed chorus of boos and cheers—but mostly cheers.

Later, in the corridor outside the Turtles' dressing room, there was an angry exchange involving Coach Wilson, several parents and Mr. Tremblay, the league commissioner. Max and Marty were surprised to see their father, Harry Mitchell, owner of the *Indian River Review*, on the perimeter of the group, listening intently and taking notes.

"Dad, what are you doing here?" Max asked.

"I was coming from the newspaper office to see the end of the hockey game," Mr. Mitchell explained. "Got here just in time to see Whizzer's tirade and his assault on the young referee."

"Assault?" asked Marty.

"Yes, assault. He struck him with a water bottle, didn't he? And cut him for stitches. And he might have speared him with a stick if you hadn't saved the day. This will be in the *Review* tomorrow. Wilson's attack was totally uncalled for. It's kids' hockey, for heaven's sake."

Whizzer Wilson, standing nearby, heard the remark and whirled to face Mr. Mitchell.

"So you're gonna crucify me in the paper?" he snarled. "After all I done for hockey in this town? I played for the town—still do—and now I'm coaching kids, teaching them the skills they need to know. And this is the thanks I get!"

"Thanks has to be earned, Whizzer," Mr Mitchell replied calmly. "Like respect. When you play for the senior team in town, you'll do anything to intimidate an opposing player. You'll break any rule—and sometimes a bone or two—to win. Tonight you lost all control and attacked the referee. That's simply not acceptable. You're a terrible role model for the boys."

Whizzer was furious. He raised a ham-like fist and took a step toward Harry Mitchell. Max stepped forward, ready to intervene if Whizzer lashed out at his dad.

"Stay back, Max!" Whizzer shouted. "I should have hammered you when I had the chance. This is none of your business!"

31

"You hit my dad and it'll be my business," Max warned Wilson. "I'll make you regret it."

Whizzer lowered his fist, hesitating. He snarled, "I mean, what happens between a coach and his players is nobody else's business."

"What happens in hockey is everybody's business," Max retorted. "Your conduct tonight was shocking. Disgraceful."

"It stank," said Marty, anxious to get in a word or two. "And don't you ever threaten our dad. I hope he tries to get you suspended."

"I intend to," Mr. Mitchell said, staring Whizzer straight in the eye.

"Oh, yeah?" Whizzer sneered, "Let me tell you— I know more about hockey than anyone. Where else in town will you find a coach as good as me?"

Mr. Mitchell didn't miss a beat. "Why, right here," he answered, waving toward Max and Marty. "Either one of my boys would be a better coach than you."

The Mitchells thought Whizzer was going to explode. He fumed and spittle ran down his lips. But he was careful not to raise a clenched fist. He knew the Mitchell brothers would be on him in a second. He pulled a key from his pocket and thrust it at Max.

"You guys are so smart," he snarled. "You think you know hockey? Here you go then. Here's the key to the Turtles' dressing room. Nobody's going to suspend me, 'cause I just quit! Now it's up to you two punks to coach those little rats, those wimps with no backbone. Why, they're so gutless they'll never win a game."

He spun on his heel and walked away.

CHAPTER 4
THE RELUCTANT VOLUNTEERS

In the lobby of the rink, Max and Marty huddled with their father.

"Thanks a lot, Dad," Marty said sarcastically. "I think you just got us appointed as coaches for the Turtles."

"I'm sorry, boys," their father said. "I didn't mean to say what I did. I was upset with Whizzer and told him the truth. I said either one of you could coach as well as he could."

"Yeah, but Mr. Tremblay, the league commissioner, overheard you," Marty said. "Right away he pumped our hands and congratulated us for volunteering. Max and I didn't know what to say. Can we still get out of it?"

"I'm sure you can," their father said. "I'll call Henry Tremblay tomorrow and explain. I'll tell him you're too busy and to find somebody else."

Just then, Max felt a tug on his sleeve. He turned to see Tim Robbins and four other Turtles standing behind him, smiling up at him.

"Is it true?" Tim asked, excited. "Is it true that you and Marty are going to be coaching us now that Mr. Wilson has quit?"

News travels fast, Max thought. He hesitated. "I don't think so, Tim," he began. "It's all a misunderstanding. Marty and I..."

The smile fell off Tim's face, replaced by a frown. His teammates looked just as glum.

"Aw, gee," Tim said sadly. "We cheered in the dressing room when we heard that you and Marty were going to coach us."

Another Turtle edged forward. "It's true," he said. "You and Marty are our favourite hockey players."

"Well, our favourite juniors," another player interjected. "We've got lots of favourites in the NHL."

A third player pleaded, "Please coach us. We'll do what you say. We'll do our best. And we won't have to listen to Mr. Wilson scream and shout at us anymore."

"And call us gutless," added another voice.

"He was an awful coach," Tim said bitterly. "Always screaming at us. We were so afraid of making mistakes. And he called us rats and scaredy-cats."

"He did?" asked Marty. "Why didn't you tell your parents?"

Tim shrugged. "I guess because we were afraid

to. He told us that we shouldn't be tattle-tales and crybabies. That we weren't to tell anyone what goes on in the dressing room."

One of the Turtles pulled on Tim's arm. "Let's go, Tim," he said. "Can't you see? Max and Marty aren't interested in us. And who can blame them? Who wants to coach a team that can't win a single game?"

"I guess you're right," Tim sighed. "Nobody's got a worse record than we do. We'll never find another coach. Not a good one. Maybe we should all quit hockey and take up skiing."

The players hefted their hockey bags to their shoulders and started to walk away, looking for their parents.

"See you," Tim called over his shoulder. "Let's go, fellows."

Max and Marty exchanged glances. Marty knew exactly what Max was thinking. "It's okay with me," he said. "Heck, it might even be fun."

That was all it took. Max grabbed Marty's arm and chased after the Turtles. "Hey, fellows!" he called out. The players turned in surprise.

"Listen, maybe we were a little hasty," Max said. "We've never coached a team before, but I think we'd like to try it."

"You mean you'll do it?" Tim Robbins said gleefully. He was so surprised his hockey bag fell off his shoulder and hit the floor with a thud.

"You'll coach the Turtles? Really?"

"Sure. Why not?" Marty said, grinning.

A wild shout echoed through the lobby. Heads turned and people laughed. Tim whooped it up with his mates. "We've got two new coaches!" he shouted.

"Max and Marty! Max and Marty! Max and Marty!" chanted his teammates.

The parents of the Turtles rushed over to hear more, and to shake hands with the Mitchell brothers.

"What great news!" one of the parents said. "You'll have so much fun coaching our kids."

"And you'll have no problems with the parents," promised the mother of one of the players. "Not like with some of the other teams in the league. We never rant and rave and get carried away—not like some parents do."

"That's right," said one of the fathers. He introduced himself as Bert Barnaby. Mr. Barnaby chuckled and said, "You won't hear us telling you who to play and when to change lines. We know our Turtles aren't that good. Heck, they may go all season without a win. Who cares as long as they have fun? Unless you fellows can pull off a coaching miracle, there's not much hope." He chuckled. "And we all know miracles don't happen very often."

"No, they don't," Max agreed. "And please don't

expect one from us. We haven't even coached before. And the season's about a third over."

"We'll have to get to know the boys," added Marty. "See what changes have to be made."

"Changes?" Suddenly, Mr. Barnaby looked concerned. "No need to make any changes. My kid Roddy is number six, the tall left winger. You'll love Roddy when you get to know him. He always gives 150 percent. The only change needed took place tonight when old Whizzer blew up like a meteor and quit the team."

Max grimaced. He disliked the cliché "150 percent." *Why did adults insist on using it?* he wondered. *Didn't they know that 100 percent was the most anyone could give?*

"Even so, teams are always changing, Mr. Barnaby," Max replied. "Players get hurt, and other players take their places. Sometimes a player plays better at one position than at another."

"Your son Roddy is a big guy," Marty added. "And a good bodychecker. I was thinking maybe he'd like it better playing defence. We'll have to see."

Mr. Barnaby hesitated before replying. Then, without much conviction, he said, "You're right, boys. Make some changes if you think they'll help. All the parents are behind you."

"Thanks, Mr. Barnaby," Marty said. "We appreciate your support."

"There's just one thing," Mr. Barnaby said. "About my son Roddy. I better come right out and tell you now."

"What's that, Mr. Barnaby?" asked Max.

"I don't *want* him playing defence," he said sharply. "Make sure you keep him on left wing. He likes to score goals, and he won't score very often as a defenceman."

Max took a deep breath. Then he said coolly, "Thanks for your opinion, Mr. Barnaby. Any changes we make will be for the good of the team."

"By the way," Marty asked, "how many goals has Roddy scored so far this season?"

"Actually, none. But he's come close a couple of times. I figure it's just a matter of time before he starts popping them in like an NHLer."

Marty almost snickered. Max glared at his brother before saying, "Thanks again, Mr. Barnaby. I hope Roddy catches fire soon."

When Mr. Barnaby walked away, Max looked at Marty. "Well, what did you think of him?"

Marty rolled his eyes. "Oh, boy," he sighed.

CHAPTER 5
FINDING A PLACE TO PRACTICE

Max and Marty received quite a shock when they called Mr. Tremblay to inquire about practice times for the Turtles. "We want to get to know the players on the team as soon as possible, Mr. Tremblay."

"Sorry, boys, but the Turtles have no practice times," Mr. Tremblay explained. "Didn't anyone tell you? Whizzer Wilson declined to take the two hours of practice time each week allotted to the teams. That time was snapped up by other clubs."

"But that's ridiculous," said Max. "How can a team win if it doesn't practice?"

"Here's what happened," said Mr. Tremblay. "Whizzer works at the mill in town, but he commutes from Turtle Creek. He built a rink in his backyard—his wife did most of the flooding—and he told his players they'd be practicing there. That way Whizzer would be able to spend more time at home with his family."

"We know where Turtle Creek is," Max said. "We

were skiing over that way the other day."

Marty said proudly, "Yep. And we saved a couple of kids from drowning. They fell through the ice."

Max steered the conversation back to hockey. "You mean the parents of the players had to drive all the way out to Turtle Creek just to get their kids to practice?"

"Yep. Couple of times a week. Some parents wouldn't do it. Some kids were driven there in an old truck with no heater. They almost froze to death."

Max was stunned. "And this was after school? When it starts to get dark?"

"Yep. But I do believe Whizzer rigged up some lighting for his rink. And he put some low boards around it."

There was a moment of silence on the phone. Then Mr. Tremblay went on. "I don't have anything against practicing outdoors, Max. But we can't have our players riding around country roads in winter. It's too dangerous. We didn't have any rules to prevent Whizzer from doing what he did, but anybody doing it now would have to get league permission—and that means permission from me."

"And there's no time available for us to practice at the arena?" Max asked once again.

"Well, we could get you an hour at 11:00 p.m., after the seniors play. Or at 5:00 a.m., before the figure skaters show up. That's it."

"No, thanks," Max replied glumly. "The parents would never agree to that. We'll have to come up with something else."

When he hung up the phone he turned to Marty. "No wonder the Turtles looked sluggish last night—they're not getting any practice. They're not in shape." But his conversation with Mr. Tremblay had given him an idea. "There's only one thing to do, Marty."

"I agree. Let's quit," Marty replied. "Get out of coaching before we run into any more problems. Call Mr. Tremblay right back. Tell him..."

"Quit? Don't be silly. We'll do what Whizzer Wilson tried to do. But we'll do it a whole lot better."

"What's that?"

"We'll bundle up and practice outdoors—on the river ice. Or maybe on the ice on some kid's back-yard rink."

"River ice is better," Marty said. "Lots more room to develop a skating stride. And you can play all day on the weekend."

"Agreed. Mr. Tremblay works for the town. I'll bet he can find a tractor with a plow to shovel off the ice. And we have a couple of old goal nets in our garage, the ones we use for street hockey games."

Marty liked the idea. "We can get them to the river in the back of Dad's truck," he said. "And maybe we can get somebody to donate some old boards to put around the rink. How about lights? If we can string a few lights the Turtles can practice after school."

That evening, they discussed the idea of an outdoor practice rink with their parents.

"It's not a bad idea," their mother said. "When your father and I were growing up, most small towns didn't have an indoor arena. Everyone skated outdoors. It was so much fun."

"That's how your mother became such a good hockey player," their father said. "She could skate like the wind. Still can. And you know she once led her team—the Snowflakes—to the Lady Stanley Cup."

"Yeah, we know, Dad," Marty said. "Mom's trophies are all over the house. There's hardly any room left for ours."

"And there's none of yours on display, Dad," Max reminded him. "Didn't you ever win one?"

"Mine are all too big to put on display," Harry Mitchell responded with a straight face. "And there are too many of them. I had to rent a large storage hall downtown to hold them all. I'll show them to you someday, but I'm far too modest to talk about them."

"Sure you are, Dad," Marty sighed.

"Tell you what I'll do," their father said. "If the parents agree, I'll mention your plans in the paper tomorrow and see if we get any reaction."

Max and Marty went back to the phone and talked with all of the parents. Almost all were willing to go along with their plans for an outdoor practice rink. Mrs. Thomas said she didn't care what the Turtles did, she was taking Chubby out of hockey. "He's not enjoying it," she told Max. "You'll have to find yourself another goalie." Max sighed and made another call. A father said, "I've got a tractor. I don't use it much in winter but it's got a plow. I'll keep that ice clear of snow for the boys."

Another said he had some surplus lumber in the shed behind his house. "We can put those old boards around the rink. They won't be high but they'll keep the puck in play—most of the time, anyway. You ever shoot a puck into a snowbank, Max? You reach in for it and the snow goes all the way up your sleeve to your armpit."

Max chuckled and said, "I've done it hundreds of times sir. Besides, low boards will force the players to shoot low. That's what we want them to do, anyway."

Chuck Robbins, Tim's father, was an avid ice fisherman. He said he'd donate a couple of old fishing huts. "I'll fix them up and throw a small stove in each one," he volunteered. "There's not enough room inside one of the huts for a full team, but two of them should be adequate." Before hanging up, he said, "Wait a second, Max.

Tim wants to talk to you."

Tim Robbins told Max he was troubled by one thing—the team's name.

"Turtles? You don't like turtles?" Max asked.

"I hate turtles! It's the stupidest name for a hockey team I ever heard. Mr. Wilson just named us Turtles because he lives in Turtle Creek. But turtles are slow and harmless. They hide under a shell. We don't want to hide. We want to be fast and tough and make other teams scared of us."

Max grinned and winked at Marty, who had a puzzled look on his face. Max put his hand over the phone and said to Marty, "Tim doesn't like the name Turtles."

"Tell him neither do we," Marty said. "It's a goofy name."

"So, Tim," Max said into the phone. "Marty and I agree. Turtles is a lousy name. You got something better?"

"I sure do," Tim said. "I talked it over with a couple of the other players. If we're going to have new coaches and a new rink we'd better come up with a new name. We want to be called the River Rats."

"River Rats?"

"Sure. Mr. Wilson often called us little rats, and it made us mad. But now we'd be proud to be known as River Rats."

CHAPTER 6

HOME OF THE RIVER RATS

The following day, Harry Mitchell's touching story in the *Indian River Review*, about the peewee team that seldom practiced, never won a game and had no goalie, drew a quick response. Readers called in to say they'd gladly help with setting up the rink boards and any shovelling that had to be done. Art Brush, a sign painter, said he'd paint some blue lines and a red line on the ice—no charge.

The strangest response was one Max and Marty received from Turtle Creek. A girl named Nicole Falzone wanted to know if the team was still looking for a goalie. When Max replied affirmatively she said, "Then I'd like to try out." She told Max she was ten years old and played in goal when her brothers and cousins skated on the pond in back of the farm she lived on. No, she'd never played on a team. Max took her phone number and told her there was a practice on Friday night at seven o'clock. Nicole told him she'd try to be there, but first she'd have to convince her father to drive her in to Indian River.

"Who was that?" Marty asked.

"Some girl named Nicole," Max answered. "Tiny little voice. Sounded really shy. She saw dad's story in the paper and wants to try out."

"I hope you told her to stay home," Marty said. "What do we know about ten-year-old girls? I don't think we want one on the team."

"We can use a goalie for our practice on Friday," Max said. "But she probably won't show. Sounds like her dad isn't too eager to drive all the way from Turtle Creek."

By Friday night, the work was complete. Max and Marty scheduled a first practice for the River Rats on Friday evening "under the lights." The ice had been swept of snow, and the red and blue lines were freshly painted. Mr. Brush had even given the goal posts and the boards a fresh coat of red paint. And a freshly painted sign had been nailed to the end of one of the fishing huts: HOME OF THE RIVER RATS.

Someone had written in chalk below: NO GIRLS ALLOWED!

Lights had been strung in two rows from posts buried in snowbanks and frozen in place with buckets of water.

A wisp of smoke rose from the L-shaped stovepipes that stuck out from the side of each fishing hut.

"Wow!" said the Mitchells.

Suddenly, small bodies in red shirts, whooping and hollering, began spilling out of the fish huts.

"Seven, eight, nine, ten," counted Marty before the doors closed behind the players who were now dashing over the ice in all directions.

"Not enough," uttered Max. "And no goalie. Mrs. Thomas meant it when she said she was taking Chubby out of hockey. One or two of the other parents must have felt the same way."

Somewhere nearby Max heard someone crying. He and Marty stepped in between the fishing huts and saw a forlorn little girl sitting on a pair of goal pads, her back against the wall.

"Hey, what's the matter?" he asked.

"They won't let me play," she wailed. "I came all the way from Turtle Creek and they won't let me play."

"Who won't let you play?" Marty asked.

"Those awful boys. The River Rats."

"You must be Nicole," Max said. "The girl who wanted a tryout." He looked around. "How did you get here? Where's your father?"

The girl wiped her nose on her sleeve and blubbered, "He went to the store. He dropped me off and told me he'd be right back. Now he won't get to see me play."

"Hey, hey, hey," Max said gently. "We're the coaches. I'm Max and this is Marty. We don't have a goalie. Get your gear on—you can play and we're glad to have you."

"But it's just a tryout," Marty said hastily. "It doesn't mean you're on the team.

The girl jumped to her feet, picked up her goal pads, flashed the brothers a grateful smile and dashed toward one of the fishing huts.

"I'll put my goal pads on in here," she said. "And if a boy tries to stop me I'll...I'll...I'll throw him in a snowbank."

After the River Rats skated around for a few minutes, warming up, Max and Marty called them to centre ice.

"No long speeches, fellows," Max began. "We're your new coaches and by the end of the hour we'll know all your names. And you'll know what my brother and I expect of you if you're going to play for the River Rats. My brother Marty plays goal for the junior team in town, so he'll be our defensive coach."

"But we don't have a goalie," someone said.

"Yes, we do," Max corrected him. "Nicole will be out on the ice in a minute..."

"Nicole? A girl? Girls can't play hockey."

"What do you mean girls can't play hockey?" Max replied. "You've all seen Trudy Reeves play, haven't you?"

"Would you prefer to protect an empty net?" Marty added. "Chubby Thomas has quit the team and we need a goalie. Nicole asked for a tryout and we're going to give her one. And no hassling her when she comes out, understand?"

Just then, Nicole came out of the hut and took her place at the back of the group. She smiled at everyone, but some of the players turned their backs on her. She shrugged.

"It's cold out here," Max said. "We want to keep you moving. We'll have some skating drills and then some passing and shooting drills. Let's go!"

Max led the peewees around the small rink in a series of drills. He threw some pucks down and gave them some simple passing and shooting drills. Nicole stood in goal and faced the shooters.

She looked nervous at first, then realized the shots she faced were no harder than the ones she handled all the time on the outdoor rink in Turtle Creek.

Her confidence soared and she began turning low shots away with ease. High shots disappeared into the big glove on her right hand.

"She looks pretty good," Max said, nudging Marty.

"So far," Marty agreed. "Somebody's been giving her hockey tips. I wonder who."

Max blew his whistle and organized a scrimmage. "We'll play four on four because we don't have a full roster," he said. "Marty will hand out some white practice shirts to some of you."

"But our side doesn't have a goalie," a player donning one of the white shirts complained. "Not fair."

"Then the other team will have to hit one of the goal posts to score," Marty told them.

Everything moved at a fast pace. Marty acted as referee and dispensed with a faceoff. He tossed the puck down the ice and yelled, "Chase it!"

The players whooped as they darted after it, each of them eager to be the first to get the puck, the first to score.

They elbowed each other out of the way, they fell down and got up, they passed and stickhandled and took wild shots on goal. It was the most fun they'd had all season and soon they were dead tired.

Max was annoyed by a couple of incidents that marred the scrimmage. Wally Wilson was overly aggressive and slammed into everyone who got in his way. He flattened Tim with a bodycheck and dumped another player over the boards into a snowbank. Concerned that one of the River Rats might be injured, Max blew his whistle.

"Take it easy, Wally!" he called out. "It's only a practice. In a real game you'd have taken two or three penalties by now."

Wally just laughed. "So? That's the way I was taught to play," he said flippantly. "If they can't take it, they should get off the ice."

Max skated over and took Wally aside. "That may be the way your uncle taught you," he said quietly, "but I want you to show more control. And I wouldn't mind a little more respect as well. From now on, this team will take fewer penalties. And that means you.

"Another thing," Max added. "I want you to stop taking so many solo dashes up the ice. Too often you get caught up there and the opposing team comes back down to score."

Wally glared at Max. "I'm the best rusher you've got," he said hotly. "Can't you see that? And the best defenceman. Why should I take orders from you? You're not much older than I am."

"Because I'm your coach," Max answered. "And my brother's your other coach. If you don't respect us, if you refuse to listen to us, perhaps you should find another team to play for. No one player is bigger than the team."

"My uncle's a great coach," Wally said. "He let me do what I want. You should, too."

"Sorry, Wally," Max sighed. "The River Rats are going to be a disciplined team from now on. You either conform to our wishes or you sit on the bench."

"Nuts to that," Wally snarled, turning to skate away. "I'm no benchwarmer. My uncle said I'd hate it playing for you two. I can be a star on any other team. So I quit."

"Fine with me," Max said.

"Oh, you'll be sorry," Wally fired back. "Just wait."

The other players had been standing around, listening. No doubt they were wondering how Max would handle their hot-tempered teammate.

Max grinned at them. "That's settled, fellows," he said. "Too bad. Wally has talent but not as much as he thinks he has. Let's get going."

The River Rats didn't say a word. But, led by Tim, they sent Max a message. One by one, they began to slap the blades of their sticks on the ice.

After ten more minutes of playing, Max called a halt. "Great effort," he praised them. "Most of you have learned the fundamentals of hockey—skating, stickhandling, passing and shooting. There's no reason Marty and I can't make winners out of you."

Marty noticed that Nicole, the goalie, was wearing tube skates like the other players.

"Don't you have goal skates, Nicole?" he asked.

"No," she replied. "My family can't afford them. I asked for some for Christmas, but..."

"Don't worry," Marty said. "I've got an old pair in the shed at home. I've outgrown them. I'll bring them next time—you can have them if they fit. And I've got a goal stick in the shed. It's better than the one you're using."

Nicole's smile lit up the ice. "You mean I can

come back?" she asked.

"Why not?" Marty laughed. "You're all we've got."

Nicole whooped with glee and dashed over to the sign on the fish hut. With a gloved hand she erased the chalked words: NO GIRLS ALLOWED!

"I see some of you are wearing hand-me-down skates," Max said. "That's okay if the skates fit. But if they're too big and you're wearing four pairs of socks to fill up the extra space, perhaps you can find a smaller pair at a skate exchange or at a rummage sale. Skates are really important. They've got to fit and the blades have got to be sharp."

"I wear my skates right over my shoes," Squirt Bragan, one of the smaller players, called out. "Look!" He pulled off his skate to reveal a worn sneaker on his foot.

Everybody began to laugh.

"I've never heard of such a thing," Marty said, snickering. "How come?"

"They're my dad's old skates," the kid answered. "Size 12."

"No wonder you're having trouble skating," Max said. "I'll talk to your dad. You've got to have skates that fit."

"And sticks must be the proper length," Marty added. "We'll show you how to measure a stick for length by putting it up to your chin. We've brought along a saw. We'll help you lop off a couple of inches if necessary."

"Now we're going to show you a few other things," Max said. "Hockey is a team game, which means we expect plenty of passing and helping each other out. We don't like players who hog the puck."

"Helping each other out means plenty of backchecking," Marty added. "Good defensive play is just as important as scoring goals."

"Let's get moving again," Max barked. "We'll show you how to get the puck out of your own zone when you're under pressure."

An hour flew by with the River Rats paying close attention to everything Max and Marty said. Finally, Max glanced at his watch and called a halt. "Your parents are waiting," he told them. "Don't linger in the dressing rooms."

As Tim Robbins skated off, he called out to the Mitchell brothers. "Best practice we've ever had," he shouted. "That was fun!"

"They're good kids," Marty concluded, after the players had hustled into the warm huts. "Eager to learn. What do you think, Max?"

"I agree. I like their attitude. There just aren't enough of them."

"That's for sure. We could use a couple more forwards, especially if we're going to move Roddy Barnaby back to defence. But all of the best peewees in town are playing with other clubs. We'll have to go with what we've got."

Just then Nicole emerged from a fish hut and approached them. "Thanks for letting me try out," she said. "All my life I've wanted to be a hockey player."

Before Max or Marty could respond they heard the blare of a horn.

"That's my dad," Nicole said, turning in the direction of a pickup truck. There were rust spots on the doors and the fenders. "Come and meet him."

A large man in a plaid mackinaw got out of the vehicle and offered an apology when they approached. "Sorry I was late getting back from the store," the man said as he shook their hands. "I'm Dino Falzone. My neighbour Silas has told me a lot about you boys."

"You're Mr. Stanowski's neighbour?" Marty asked.

"That's right. Thanks for letting Nicole skate with your team. Last time she played was on the Stanowski pond. His twin boys almost drowned that day."

"So that was you on the ice when the twins fell through?" Marty asked, looking at Nicole. "You sure ran home in a hurry."

"I was scared," Nicole said. "And Mr. Stanowski had a shotgun."

Mr. Falzone said, "I told Nicole this was a wild goose chase, bringing her all the way in from Turtle Creek. Obviously she's not ready for organized hockey. Nobody wants a girl on a team."

"Wait a minute, Mr. Falzone," Max said, holding up a gloved hand to stop the flow of words. "Nicole did really well. We want her on our team. The question is, can you get her here for games and practices? Are you willing to make a commitment to us?"

The man was stunned. "Really? She made the team." He began to chuckle. "Well, how about that. It was always her dream to play on a team. I can't believe..." He gazed proudly at his daughter. "She doesn't even have goal skates. Or a decent stick. And I can't afford..."

"We've already taken care of that," Marty told him.

"If you're willing to let her play for the River Rats, we'll need your name, address and phone number," Max told him. "And your signature on this form."

"Sure, I'll make a commitment," the man said. He looked at the form and then frowned. "There's just one thing," he said in a whisper. "Nicole's got a real pretty face. I worry about her getting hit by a puck or stick in organized hockey. Any thoughts on that?"

It was Marty who came up with a suggestion.

"Max and I play baseball in the summer. I'm a catcher, so I wear a mask. Sometimes I wear it in goal, too. How about I let Nicole borrow it for the rest of the season? That may work."

"Sounds good to me," Dino Falzone said, reaching for a pen. "Where do I sign?"

"We hope to practice here a couple of times a week," Max told Mr. Falzone. "Is that going to be a problem?"

"Hmmm. It could be. I've got a farm to run, just down the road from Silas. That's a lot of running back and forth. I can't promise to get Nicole here every time. It's too much..."

Max snapped his fingers. "I just thought of something!" he interrupted. "Nicole's friends, Lance and Larry, are good little players. We could use two more kids on the team. If we could get them to play for the River Rats, you and Mr. Stanowski could take turns driving them to games and practices. And maybe Joe Stanowski could help out."

"But, Max," Marty remonstrated. "You've forgotten. Silas Stanowski has barred the twins from hockey for a couple of weeks. Don't you remember?"

"Marty, he banned them from pond hockey—not from playing in a league. And he said he'd do anything for us, didn't he?"

Max turned to Mr. Falzone. "Why don't you talk

to Mr. Stanowski? We'll give him a call, too. If his twins want to play for us, we'd love to have them."

It was Max's final persuasive argument that sank home. "It may even help them deal with the loss of their mother."

When Mr. Falzone drove away and the Mitchell brothers headed for home, a sinister-looking figure stepped out from behind a large tree. He'd been watching the River Rats work out on their new rink.

"Those Mitchell kids think they're so smart," he muttered to himself. "Wait'll they find out what I've got in store for them. They won't know what hit them."

CHAPTER 7

WINNERS AT LAST

One Saturday morning, the River Rats, under the direction of two new coaches—Max and Marty Mitchell—and with three new faces in their line-up, played a league game indoors at the Indian River Arena. A sizeable crowd turned out—at least 100 people—to see the team perform against the Steamrollers, the best club in the four-team league.

Some of the fans came out to see the league's only female player, Nicole Falzone, make her debut. Others came to see Silas Stanowski's twin sons suit up for the River Rats.

"Three good players can often turn a team around," Silas Stanowski said to Max and Marty in the corridor before the game. "Doesn't matter if it's an NHL team or a peewee team. I hope my Lance and Larry—and Nicole—can do that for you."

"We want to thank you for allowing your sons to play for the River Rats," Max told him. "They fit in well. I think they're enjoying it."

"They are," Mr. Stanowski admitted. "At first, I didn't want them playing on a team. Getting involved in all that nonsense that goes on in minor hockey. Parents squabbling and shrieking, coaches who want to win at all costs. Some coaches can't teach because they've never played the game. Some coaches give their sons a lot more ice time than the other kids on the team. I figured my kids would have more fun on the backyard pond."

"I hope you approve of what we're doing," Marty said. "If you have any suggestions..."

"I do approve," Mr. Stanowski said hastily. "You boys are good instructors. I like the way you keep the fun in the game. And because you're still young, nobody can say you favour your sons over the other players."

"That's true," Max said. "And I hope you don't mind the long drive in from Turtle Creek. It helps when Mr. Falzone brings Nicole and the twins. It means less driving for you."

"It does," Mr. Stanowski agreed. "But I've got to admit I enjoy seeing the lads play. So you'll be seeing me at most of the games. And that Nicole! She's a humdinger in goal."

Mr. Stanowski shifted a bundle of books that he held in his arm.

"Where'd you get the books?" Marty asked.

Mr. Stanowski chuckled. "One good thing about coming in to town is the library. I've rediscovered reading since my wife passed away. I drop the kids off for practice, then scoot over to the library for half an hour."

"Then you've met Miss Fallis, our librarian. She's a great lady," Max said. "Marty and I enjoy reading, too."

"I love the Hardy Boys books," Marty added.

Silas Stanowski didn't seem impressed by Marty's announcement. "Miss Fallis has been very helpful," he said. "Every book she's recommended has been a good one."

"Hey, it's almost game time," Marty said. "Let's go."

The Steamrollers were rough and arrogant. They had won six in a row since the opening of the season and they taunted the River Rats during the pre-game warm-up. Their best player—and their roughest—was Bert "Bully Boy" Butcher, a tall defenceman with a quick temper.

"Changed yer team's name, did ya?" Butcher shouted at Tim Robbins in the pre-game warm-up. He circled the ice, moving closer to Tim, almost bumping him. "Shoulda changed it to Pussycats," he sneered. "Har har har. And you've sunk so low you had to put a girl in goal. What's that crazy thing she's wearing on her face. Doesn't matter—she'll cry her eyes out when I blast a few shots at her."

Tim said nothing. Max and Marty had stressed penalty-free hockey. "Stay cool! Don't retaliate!"

they had cautioned. "And don't argue with the referee. Nobody yet has scored a goal from the penalty box."

The Mitchell brothers had examined the stats of past games and discovered a long list of unnecessary penalties picked up by the Turtles under Whizzer Wilson. The team had played short-handed far too often.

"Coach Wilson told us to whack a player back and never turn the other cheek when we got hit," Tim had explained. "He showed us a lot of dirty tricks. If we didn't use them he benched us and called us sissies. We always got lots more penalties than the team we were playing."

"Retaliation penalties are bad penalties," Max had told them. "They show a lack of discipline."

The referee was about to drop the puck to start the game when a howl echoed through the arena. A man bolted from his seat and charged down the steps to rinkside.

"Max! Max!" he shouted. "You've made a mistake. You've got Roddy on defence. Put him back at left wing where he belongs!"

It was Mr. Barnaby, and he was enraged.

"Teenagers never listen," he turned to bellow at the crowd. "I told young Mitchell my boy plays left wing." He pointed toward Roddy, who was standing quietly on the blue line. "Now look where he's got him."

"Roddy! Roddy!" he shouted. "Play up on left wing!"

Max was embarrassed. He was in his first game as a coach, and the game hadn't even begun before he had to deal with an irate father. He moved quickly to the end of the bench and motioned for Mr. Barnaby to come closer.

When he did, Max said quietly but firmly, "Please go back to your seat, Mr. Barnaby. And don't interfere. Your son and I agreed that he should play defence—at least for the time being."

"But I don't *want* him on defence," Mr. Barnaby insisted. "He's a left winger. I told you that."

"Mr. Barnaby, you're holding up the game. It's not about what you want. It's about what Roddy and I want. I'm the coach and he's the player. Look at Roddy! He's squirming. You've embarrassed him."

Roddy could stand still no longer. He skated over, his face beet red.

"Dad! Go and sit down!" he croaked. Roddy's throat was dry, his face was red. He was mortified, trembling with emotion.

Max echoed Roddy's comment. "Sit down, Mr. Barnaby," he said sharply. "Don't ever do this again."

Fuming, Mr. Barnaby turned and made his way back to his seat. The other spectators began discussing the incident, and there was a smattering of applause. Max could only hope it was for him and not the angry parent.

Someone in the crowd bellowed, "Put a sock in it, Barnaby! Quit interfering!"

Then the game was underway and the Steamrollers sent an instant message to the River Rats: We're out to win our seventh straight and there's not a thing you can do about it. They had speed and confidence and within two minutes they had their first goal. Bert Butcher drilled a long shot at Nicole. The puck deflected off a stick and wound up in the net behind her.

"Yahoo!" roared Butcher, raising his arms in the air. "There's more where that came from, sister," he sneered.

Darn it, Nicole said to herself, *I was hoping for a shutout today. Marty's old skates and pads fit me like a glove. I'm not nervous and those boys on the Steamrollers don't scare me.* She banged her stick on the ice. "Come on, guys!" she shouted to her teammates. "That's just one goal. Let's get it back."

But the River Rats didn't get it back. They came close, but every time they moved in on Terry Riley, the Steamrollers' goalie, there was a penalty. Two minutes for slashing. Two minutes for holding. Two minutes for interference. By the end of the second period, the River Rats had been penalized ten times, the Steamrollers only once.

"There's something funny going on," Marty said

to Max during the intermission. "Our boys are playing clean hockey, the Steamrollers aren't—especially young Butcher—and we're getting all the penalties."

"Thank goodness the Stanowski twins are with us," Max replied. "They've killed off most of the penalties with their stickhandling and passing skills. We still trail by just one goal."

"The referee stinks," Marty said bluntly. "I think he's biased."

Marty strode over to the scorer's table and talked briefly with the scorekeeper.

He came back fuming.

"Guess what?" he said to Max. "The referee is Bill Wilson, brother of Whizzer Wilson. I get it now. Whizzer wants to see us lose every game. And he's got his brother to help make it happen."

In a flash, Max took off down the corridor to the officials' dressing room. The referee and linesman were just emerging, butting out cigarettes, ready to take the ice for the final period.

"Wilson!" Max barked. "Wait a second."

The referee, a young man in his early twenties, turned and said, "What do you want, Coach?"

"I want fairness," Max retorted angrily. "Your brother put you up to this, didn't he?"

"My brother wants nothing to do with you or your team," Wilson snapped back.

"Good. Then there's no good reason for you to

give us all the penalties," Max said. "Come on, Wilson, you're hurting a lot of good kids with your calls tonight. I've seen you referee before and you're good. But tonight your bias stands out like a beacon. You're hurting the game and you're hurting yourself. Kids look up to referees, they respect them. But you've earned no respect tonight. Think about it."

The third period got underway and the Steamrollers began to worry about their winning streak. One goal wasn't much of a lead against a bunch of eager kids who could skate with them and were strong defensively. The girl in goal was a major surprise—she could stop pucks—and the big defenceman, Roddy Barnaby, cleared loose pucks and displayed a love of body contact. He stepped into every forward wearing a sweater with the big steamroller logo stitched to the front. And he taught Bert Butcher a valuable lesson—keep your head up. Butcher led a rush and dropped a pass to a teammate. Then he turned to admire the pass, and that's when Barnaby nailed him with a crushing bodycheck.

Wham! Butcher flew backwards and landed on his backside. The whistle stopped play when Butcher failed to get up. He lay there for a full minute, the wind knocked out of him.

"No penalty. Clean check," the referee ruled as he helped pull Butcher to his feet.

His teammates escorted Butcher to their bench. Losing his breath had frightened him, and there were tears in his eyes.

Tim skated by the Steamrollers' bench and asked innocently, "You're not crying, are you, Butch? I thought you were going to make our goalie cry?"

Butcher groaned and wiped his eyes.

"Leave him alone," snarled the opposing coach.

In previous games, the River Rats, formerly the Turtles, wilted in the third period. Lack of conditioning and lack of depth left them gasping. But the outdoor practice sessions were paying off. By the five-minute mark, the Steamrollers began to huff and puff. And they obviously missed the intimidating presence of Bully Boy Butcher.

Midway through the period, the Steamrollers began to complain to the referee. Their coach, a mouthy man with a cigar jammed into his mouth, hollered across the ice, "Come on, Ref, give them a penalty. What happened, you swallow your whistle?"

The referee glared at him and barked, "One more comment and you'll get the penalty."

Max overheard the comment and smiled. Perhaps his chat with the referee between periods had done some good.

Marty had noticed something. "The Stanowski twins are too fast for the third player on their line," he told Max. "He can't keep up. We're losing scoring chances because of it."

Max respected Marty's opinion and made a quick change. He moved Tim Robbins to centre on a line with the twins.

Bingo! The line clicked immediately. Robbins, a fine passer, fed the puck to Lance Stanowski, who flipped it over to his brother Larry. Larry barged in on the Steamrollers' defence and dropped the puck to Tim, who drilled the disc through three sets of legs only to see his shot clang off the goal post. But Lance was there to corral the rebound and whip the puck into the net behind Riley.

Red light! An explosion of cheers from the stands as the River Rats supporters leaped from their seats, applauding noisily.

"River Rats! River Rats! River Rats!"

Max and Marty could hear Trudy's voice above the others.

"Great play, Tim! Nice goal, Lance!"

The River Rats beamed collectively as they touched gloves and marvelled at the crowd reaction.

"That's the biggest cheer we've ever heard," an awestruck Tim Robbins said to Lance.

"Want to hear a louder one? Score another goal," Lance advised him.

A few minutes later, Tim heeded that bit of advice.

He led a rush down the ice, flanked by the

Stanowski twins. The puck slipped from one stick to another, confusing the defenders. Tim passed off to Lance, slipped between the floundering defencemen, took a return pass and fired the puck—all in one motion. He was bowled over just as he got the shot away and failed to see what happened. But the roar of the crowd told him he'd scored! Then he was buried under his teammates who pounded him on the back and shoulders. "Way to go, Timmeee! Way to go!"

Tim worked his way out from under the pile and glanced up at the clock. One minute to play.

"It's the first time this season we've held a lead," he murmured to himself. "Now we've got to hold on for the win."

He glanced at the bench and saw Max pointing at the faceoff circle and nodding. He and the twins would play the final 60 seconds.

The Steamrollers worked frantically to tie the score. They even pulled their goalie for an extra attacker, a rare bit of strategy in 1936. But Tim and the Stanowski kids played standout defensive hockey and held the Steamrollers to one shot on goal. Nicole turned it aside and Roddy Barnaby hoisted the puck down the ice as time ran out and the celebration began.

Max and Marty whooped with joy and embraced each other. "What a feeling!" Marty shouted in Max's ear. "Our first win as coaches!"

"Yep. It's almost as much fun as playing," Max replied, pounding Marty on the back.

On the ice, the River Rats raced over to congratulate Nicole on her sparkling play. Then they wheeled around to line up for the traditional post-game handshake with the Steamrollers.

But their opponents were gone!

"I can't believe it," Marty snorted. "Their coach yanked them off the ice. What a poor loser! And look! He flipped his cigar butt at us before he left the rink."

"Remind me to talk to the league president about that," Max said. "Coaches shouldn't be allowed to smoke inside the arena. Neither should the referees. I'm going to suggest they make it a rule."

"What about the parents?" Marty asked. "You want them to butt out, too?"

"That would be good," Max answered. "But let's take it one step at a time."

The last word went to the referee, Bill Wilson. Before leaving the ice, he skated past the River Rats' bench.

"Nice game, you guys," he said out of the corner of his mouth.

CHAPTER 8

PROBLEMS WITH PARENTS

Practices twice a week on the river ice did wonders for the River Rats. In the next two weeks they reeled off a four-game win streak and found themselves alone in second place—behind the Steamrollers—in the league standings.

Max and Marty schooled the boys on hockey's fundamentals. Skating drills often took them outside the confines of the rink. With Max and Marty leading the way, the boys and Nicole, who threw aside her goal pads, set off on mile-long dashes over the river ice, learning to push and glide, push and glide.

"A lot of NHLers are called 'river skaters' because they learned to skate this way," Max told his players. "They have long, easy strides that make them look fast and smooth."

Back on the rink, the boys were told that puck possession was all-important. "If you have the puck, the other team can't score," Marty emphasized. "So win the faceoffs and control the puck.

Force the other team to take it away from you."

There were dozens of tips on team play and individual performance: how to clear the zone, how to kill a penalty, how to control the puck on a power play. Players were taught to skate and stickhandle with their heads up. They were taught how to shoot the puck properly and how to cradle their stick blades to receive sharp passes.

And they were told repeatedly, "You're here to have fun. If you don't have fun, what's the sense of playing?"

During one session, Max injected some fun into a drill by bringing Big Fella onto the ice and parking him in front of the goal. Behind the net, a River Rat defenceman tried to pull Big Fella out of position by moving the puck back and forth before starting out on a rush. Big Fella scrambled from side to side, daring the defenceman to move out. Afterwards, in the dressing room, Max told his forwards, "See, Big Fella was smart enough not to dash in behind the net and get caught. I want you to do the same, okay?"

One of the Stanowski twins came up with the perfect response. "Ruff! Ruff!" he barked.

Max laughed along with everybody else. He was glad to see the twins coming out of their shell.

But a show of impish humour was uncommon behaviour from the two boys. Lance and Larry were deeply affected by the loss of their mother.

On the team bench, they often sat with their heads down, not really focused on the game.

"They look so sad," Trudy observed. "So dejected. I wish there was something we could do for them."

"There's not much we can do," Max sighed. "Except be patient. Time will heal some of the hurt. But it must be devastating to lose your mother."

"I saw their big brother Joe the other night," Marty said. "He drove the boys in to town for practice. Then he disappeared until it was time to pick them up. He's a strange bird."

Max nodded his head in agreement. "I can't figure him out. I don't think he likes sports. And you never see him hanging out at Merry Mabel's with the rest of the high-school kids. Oh well, to each his own."

The Mitchell brothers were surprised to see Miss Fallis, the librarian, at the River Rats' next game. Miss Fallis had never shown any interest in sports. They bumped into her in the crowded lobby prior to the game.

"Miss Fallis!" Marty exclaimed. "How good to see you. I didn't know you were a hockey fan. You here to cheer for a relative?"

She blushed and hesitated before answering. "No, I'm here to see the sons of a friend of mine. Lance and Larry Stanowski. Their father tells me they're good little players."

"Their father's right," Marty said. "They're a joy to watch and a joy to coach."

After the game, Miss Fallis took Max by the arm. "I've never been so excited in my life. Watching the River Rats was so much fun. I think I've been spending too much time in the library. Max, if you ever need help with the team, I'll gladly volunteer."

Max walked her to her car. "Thanks, Miss Fallis," he said. "Wow! What a big car you're driving."

She smiled. "My father left it to me when he died. He owned the Fallis Funeral Home, you know. It's far too big for me. And it's a little embarrassing driving around in a hearse. But it's in perfect shape and it carries a lot of memories of my father. I guess I'll keep it until I find something smaller."

"Before you go, Miss Fallis, do you mind if I ask you something?"

"Anything, Max."

"Well, Marty and I were talking about Joe Stanowski the other day, and how he doesn't fit in with the other kids in town. You know the Stanowski family, and we were wondering..."

"I know. You were wondering if Joe's an oddball, somewhat anti-social—a bit peculiar?"

"That's it, I guess."

"Let me tell you, Max—Joe is not your normal teenager. He has no interest in sports or hanging out after school. But he has a brilliant mind and an incredible thirst for knowledge. He spends every free minute studying. He's always after me for the latest books on science and mathematics. He wants to grow up fast and become a success— so that he can help his dad and his brothers have an easier life. I'm so impressed with Joe. He's so...so gifted."

Max was stunned. The mysterious Joe Stanowski, the loner who dressed in oddball clothes, the non-athlete who never mingled with the other kids at school, was gifted? Max knew that Joe was smart and always received top grades. But he was also the kid other teens snickered at and called "alien" and "nerd".

"While you and your friends are listening to the jukebox and having fun at Merry Mabel's," Miss Fallis said, "Joe Stanowski is poring over science and math books, absorbing important information that will take him far in this world one day. I'm certain of it."

"That's incredible," Max replied. "Marty and I thought..."

Miss Fallis smiled. "I know. You thought he was a bit weird. That's understandable. Most people look at Joe that way. But Max, we can't all be athletes like you and Marty. And we can't all be social butterflies. Some of us are destined to be different. Young men and women like Joe march to a different drummer, and there's nothing wrong with that. In fact, I think it's admirable."

"Thanks, Miss Fallis," Max said enthusiastically. "Thanks for that. You've really enlightened me. We had Joe pegged all wrong. From now on I'll show him a lot more respect. And I'd like to sit down with him one day, you know, and get to know him. I'm interested in science myself."

"Then you should do it, Max, and do it soon. First thing you know, Joe will be off to college. After that, I have a hunch he's going to make a big mark in the world. And you'll be able to say with pride, 'I knew Joe Stanowski when he lived in Indian River. He's a friend of mine.'"

Max walked away smiling. Perhaps he'd give Joe Stanowski a call later in the week. Invite him over to the house for some brownies and hot chocolate, and show him the project he was working on for the science fair in the spring.

Max and Marty were often shocked by the behaviour of some of the parents who attended the games.

One night, the mother of a player on a rival team blew a whistle during a three-on-one rush against her son, who was the goalie. The first time she did it the River Rats stopped skating, thinking the referee had stopped play. An opposing player stole the puck, raced off in the other direction and scored!

"I can't believe she did that," Max fumed, looking up in the stands. "That cost us a goal."

During the intermission, he approached the woman and told her he thought her behaviour was inappropriate. He could barely control his temper.

She laughed in his face. "Listen, sonny, anything goes in hockey," she told him. "I'll do what I want."

Her husband, who was sitting next to her, lumbered to his feet. He was a big man, over 200 pounds.

"What are you butting in for?" he asked, pushing Max in the chest, knocking him backwards. "Mind yer own business."

Max regained his balance and angrily pushed back—hard. The man fell back in his seat, gasping, the breath knocked out of him.

Max snorted. "Some parents you are! We teach the kids to play fair and respect their opponents, and it's the parents who turn out to be the cheaters. Why not throw that whistle away? You know it's not right to blow it during a game."

She smirked, and replied by blasting it in his ear.

He walked away, red-faced in frustration.

The Mitchell brothers were also disturbed by some of the verbal abuse directed at players by parents in the stands. And it came from behind both benches.

"Get up, you little so-and-so! Don't take that from him! Get up and smack him!"

"Murray, stay onside! Don't you listen? Don't you know anything? You go offside one more time and you'll get no allowance this week."

"Wake up, Norman! Make hard passes! Hard passes! How many times do I have to tell you?"

Max said to Marty, "Let's get the parents together in the dressing room. We'll ask them to stop bombarding their kids with criticism. The players need to hear more encouraging words. Marty, we're lucky our parents always supported us as pee-wees, and still do. Murray Marshall told me he dreads the ride home with his folks after a game. He knows he's going to hear about all the mistakes he made."

"Sure, Murray makes mistakes," Marty said. "All our kids do. But they do a lot of things well, and they're having fun. Some of their folks are great. But Murray's dad said to me the other day, 'How many of the River Rats will we see in the NHL some day, Marty?' I told him likely none."

"How did he react?" asked Max.

"Turned on his heel and walked away. I know he thinks Murray is going to make it to pro hockey.

He told me, 'But only if he listens to his dad.'"

Max shook his head. "Some parents..." he began. "Sounds like Murray's dad is hoping his son will have the career he never had."

One time, a young referee was having trouble handling the game. He struggled making penalty calls. Sometimes he waited too long to blow his whistle and make the call. At other times he ignored the penalty altogether. By the end of the game, one woman was so incensed that she rushed down to rinkside and swung her purse at the young man, striking him on the shoulder. Then her purse fell to the ice.

The official groaned and fell to one knee. He clutched his shoulder and winced in pain.

A linesman skated over and helped the referee to his feet. When the linesman collected the purse, a heavy rock tumbled out of it and bounced along the ice. He turned, seeking the owner, but she had disappeared in the crowd.

Within a month of taking over as coaches, Max and Marty had to deal with a problem they hadn't anticipated. Chubby Thomas, whose mother had yanked him from the team, wanted to come back.

"My mom says she's much happier with you guys coaching," Chubby said when he showed up at the rink one day. "I didn't really want to quit. My mom told me to."

"But we have another goalie now," Max

explained. "Nicole is playing great in goal. We can't give you her position."

Chubby was crestfallen. "I know, I know," he said. "I figured you'd say that."

He turned to walk away.

Marty said, "Wait, Chubby. It's true we can't let you replace Nicole. But I've seen you skate. Do you think you could play another position for us— like defence?"

Chubby's face broke into a grin. "Sure, I could play defence. I'm too awkward in goal anyway. With all that padding and stuff." He patted his ample stomach. "I've got enough padding already."

"Well, we've got one position open," said Max. "And that's on defence. Want to give it a try?"

"Just give me a chance," Chubby said. "I'll really surprise you."

And he did. Chubby was surprisingly fast on his skates, and he was good at clearing the puck from in front of the net.

"He's strong—strong enough to knock opponents down. And strong enough to bang the puck down the ice," Max observed. "He's a keeper."

Mrs. Thomas was not as happy as her son. She phoned Max one night. "When I told Chubby he could return to hockey, I thought surely you'd put him back in goal," she chided. "His father was a goalie and he wants his son to be a goalie. We invested in goal pads, spent almost 20 dollars on equipment."

"I'm sorry, Mrs. Thomas," Max said politely. "But Nicole is now our goalie. If Chubby hadn't quit...no, I'll say it. If Chubby hadn't been pulled from the team..."

Mrs. Thomas ignored the comment. "But Nicole is just a girl. Why in the world would you put a girl in goal? She can't be very good."

"She is good," Max argued. He almost added what he was thinking: *Much better than Chubby.* Instead he said, "If Nicole gets injured or if she's sick, it'll be good to have Chubby around. You know, as a backup."

"I can see you're a stubborn young man, Max Mitchell," Mrs. Thomas said angrily. "Perhaps Chubby would be better off out of hockey after all."

"That's your decision, Mrs. Thomas. But I hope you won't do that. Chubby gets along well with the other fellows. He's popular. And he's a good defenceman. If you pull him out of hockey again, it might not be easy for him to get back. You'd be robbing him of a lot of fun."

CHAPTER 9

PRACTICAL JOKERS

Nobody had more fun that winter than Marty. Not only did he enjoy coaching the River Rats, he entertained them with funny stories and poems. And he had a captive audience.

"Here's a couple of poems from the famous poet Anon," he told them.

There was a young lady from Lynn
Who was so excessively thin
That when she essayed
To drink lemonade
She slipped through the straw and fell in.

Encouraged by the players' laughter and applause, he continued.

When the donkey saw the zebra,
He began to twitch his tail.
"Well, I never!" said the donkey,
"There's a mule that's been to jail."

But the biggest laugh came after Marty puffed out his chest and bragged, "People say I spread happiness *wherever* I go."

Squirt Bragan came up with the perfect squelch. "No, Marty, they say whenever you go."

And it was Squirt who almost upstaged Marty with a couple of jokes.

"My kid sister Francine was in art class, and she told the teacher she was drawing a picture of God. The teacher said, 'But Francine, nobody knows what God looks like.'

"So my sister said, 'They will in a minute when I get this finished.'

"Then the teacher asked Francine, 'If a fire broke out in the art gallery, and you could save only one painting, which one would it be?'

"My sister said, 'The one nearest the exit.'"

Then Tim Robbins chipped in with some unexpected wit.

"Did you know I fell over 50 feet this afternoon?"

The boys grinned, waiting for the punch line.

"I wasn't hurt, but I've never had so much trouble getting off the school bus," Tim finished, nudging Squirt with his elbow and knocking him off the end of the bench.

Gales of laughter echoed off the walls of the fish hut as the boys took turns trying to make each other laugh.

Max didn't contribute, but he stood back and

watched. He could see the team was bonding and it pleased him.

A few days later, Marty masterminded one of the season's most memorable practical jokes.

At one practice session, the young mother of one of the players brought her one-year-old baby to the rink.

"I don't have a babysitter," she told Marty. "And I may have to feed my baby and change her diaper while I'm waiting for my son."

"I understand, Mrs. Brown," Marty said. "You can use one of the dressing rooms. They're very warm. When the team is out on the ice you'll have plenty of privacy."

Later, he saw Mrs. Brown enter the dressing room with her baby. When she came out, she was holding a paper bag. She was somewhat embarrassed. "I'm not sure how to dispose of this," she said. "The soiled diaper is inside."

"No problem, Mrs. Brown," Marty said. "I'll get rid of it for you."

She thanked him and took her baby to the car.

Marty sniffed the bag and muttered, "Yuck." Then he slipped into the dressing room, found his brother's hockey bag and tucked the diaper into a far corner.

Two days passed before Max discovered the diaper. The team was preparing to practice when he plucked it from his hockey bag and asked,

"What's this?" He made a face and held his nose before he opened the bag.

"Yikes!" he bellowed, fanning his face. "What a stench! All right. Which one of you mutts did this?"

Nobody answered. They were laughing too hard.

"I'll get even," Max vowed. "I am the master of the practical joke. Just you wait."

A week later, the boys were scraping snow off the rink when they heard the beep of a car horn. They looked up to see the flashing lights of Sheriff Jake Braddock's police cruiser. The sheriff beeped the horn a second time and called them over. The sheriff, normally an easygoing chap with an engaging smile, was tight-lipped and grim.

"Uh oh! Something's up," Max whispered to Marty as the River Rats gathered around. "We may be in trouble." The sheriff stared at them icily, then delivered a curt message.

"Judge Gaul wants to see you fellows in his office—at once!"

"Judge Gaul!" gasped the River Rats. They had heard all about Judge Gaul. Some of their parents referred to the magistrate as "Hanging" Judge Gaul. He was a no-nonsense judge, known throughout the North Country for the stiff sentences he handed out to lawbreakers.

A heavy-set, middle-aged man with a florid complexion and a perpetual scowl on his face,

Judge Gaul was thought to be devoid of a sense of humour. It was said that his face was as long and harsh as the sentences he handed out.

"Let's go, fellas," Max urged. "The judge hates to be kept waiting."

Alarmed, the boys dropped their shovels and rushed down Main Street. A couple of them muttered, "We're in for it now. But what did we do wrong?"

"We'll find out soon enough," Max replied. "Try to pull yourselves together and hope for the best."

They climbed the stairway to the judge's office in the town hall. Max knocked on the large oak door.

"Come in!" boomed a basso profundo voice, and the younger boys all but squealed in fear.

"Hush! Be brave!" Max commanded them before they shuffled into the room.

The judge turned a scowling face toward them as he moved away from his roll top desk. Marty thought he detected a small black cloud hovering over Judge Gaul's head.

"Who speaks for this group?" he demanded.

The boys quickly pointed at Max. "He does," they murmured in unison.

"Oh, I don't think so," the judge contradicted. "No, not Max Mitchell. He's no criminal. I know his family well—all but his brother Marty." Judge Gaul raised a bony finger. "Which one of you is he?"

Marty gulped. *Criminal? What crime was the old judge talking about?* he thought. His heart was racing, and a drop of perspiration dripped from his brow onto his nose.

"That would be me," he blurted through trembling lips. "I'm Marty, Your Highness, I mean Your Judgeship...I mean Your Lord...I mean Your Honour."

Max turned his head away, suppressing a smile.

Judge Gaul pointed that long bony finger straight at Marty.

"Tell me," he growled. "Do you and the rest the rascals in this room have a licence to construct a rink on the river? If you do, let's see it." He waved his hand, as if he expected Marty to produce some sort of legal paper or document.

"Yes, sir. I mean, no, sir," Marty mumbled. "The only licence I have is for Big Fella, our pet husky. A dog licence. About a rink licence...we didn't know..."

"Ignorance of the law is no excuse," the judge thundered, slapping one hand on his desk. He looked around. "Do you have a licence?" he asked, glaring at Squirt.

Squirt jumped. "No, sir," he said, through trembling lips.

The judge moved around his desk. The River Rats shrank back.

Calmly, Max stepped forward. "Your Honour, I must confess it was my idea to build a rink on the river for the River Rats. I'll have to take full responsibility. Sir, we didn't think we needed a licence."

Judge Gaul's stern look appeared to soften. A hint of a smile pursed his lips, and his piercing eyes displayed a rare sparkle.

Marty and the River Rats breathed a sigh of relief. Max was going to get them off the hook.

"And a great idea it is," roared the judge. He burst out laughing. "I'm proud of you, Max. As for your brother, well, I've got something for you, young man."

He picked up a thick cane from behind his back and whacked it on the desk. Twice.

Marty leaped back a foot, thinking he was about to be caned.

"There's a fly in here," the judge bellowed. "Can't stand flies." He whacked the desk again, and some legal documents flew through the air.

"Step forward, Marty."

Marty gulped and took a step forward.

"Take this!" the judge ordered, thrusting out what appeared to be a white towel.

Marty reached out. To his amazement, the judge unrolled the towel. But it was no towel—it was a baby's diaper.

Some of the River Rats snickered. Then they

burst out laughing.

"I hear you're fond of such underwear," Judge Gaul chuckled. "So wear it proudly."

He extended his other hand and slipped a ten-dollar bill into Marty's palm.

"You boys get out of here. Scat! Go down to Merry Mabel's and buy yourselves some hamburgers. Compliments of the 'Hanging' Judge and my friend Max, the king of the practical jokers."

The boys bounced from the room and tumbled down the stairs. Behind them they could hear a roar of laughter and the sound of a cane whacking a desk.

Max was the last to leave. As he closed the door, he looked back and winked at the judge.

"That was a good one, Your Honour," he said quietly, giving the judge a thumbs up. "You scared the pants off of them—especially Marty."

"It was a great practical joke, Max. It brightened my day."

Sooner than he could have imagined, Max would find himself in the same courtroom with Judge Gaul for the second time. On this occasion they'd be dealing with a far more serious matter. Both could only wish it was all a practical joke.

CHAPTER 10
BACK IN JUDGE GAUL'S COURTROOM

Max was sweeping the dressing-room floor at the arena. The game was over—another win for the River Rats—and the players had dispersed.

Using a dustpan, Max scooped up loose tape and some wood chips from a broken stick and threw them in a garbage can. He dusted off his hands and turned to Marty.

"We've got to drop Danny Winters from the River Rats," he said grimly.

"But why?" Marty said. "He's not a bad player."

"Not bad. But he's not giving us his best. And he's not doing well in school. I talked to his teacher and..."

"And?"

"She told me Danny's a lazy student. A failing student. Remember, we told the players they'd have to keep their marks up if they wanted to play with the River Rats. We've got to live up to that promise."

"I guess you're right," Marty said. "But his

father is going to be furious. He dotes on Danny. Says he's going to play in the NHL someday."

"Well, he's not. Not unless he learns how to apply himself, on and off the ice. And his father's a pain in the butt. He insists on being in the dressing room at all times. He refused to leave the other night when I asked the parents to wait outside while we had a pre-game meeting. And he's angry with us because we don't use Danny on the power play."

"Oh, boy," Marty muttered. "We're going to get an earful from Danny's father over this."

The Mitchell brothers got more than an earful from Mr. Winters. He accosted them in the arena lobby the following day.

"You young pups know nothing about coaching," he accused them. "You just dropped the best player on your team. My boy is devastated. He may have a nervous breakdown over this blow...this rejection."

"Danny knew our rules," Max said quietly. "Our players have to maintain a passing grade in school. And Danny..."

"How can he do that when you treat him like garbage?" Mr. Winters roared. "You ignore him. You don't play him enough. You insult him by not putting him on the power play. You may have destroyed his chances for a big-league career. No wonder he's doing poorly at school."

Max and Marty exchanged glances. Were they really guilty? Hadn't they treated Danny like all the other team members? Hadn't they given him every chance to succeed, to prove himself?

"Mr. Winters..." Marty began.

"Oh, shut up," the irate parent bellowed. "I've heard enough and seen enough. I'm retaining a lawyer. I'll see you in court."

Mr. Winters stormed off.

"Did he really say he was getting a lawyer?" Marty said, bewildered.

"That's what he said," Max grunted. "Now we're going to be dragged into court. And all because we decided to drop a player from our roster."

Mr. Winters was true to his word. He hired a lawyer who brought charges against Max and Marty. They were accused of "wilfully and wrongfully damaging the psyche and emotions of Danny Winters, a member of the River Rats, of destroying the sensitive player's morale, self-confidence and self-esteem to the point where his performance in school suffered terribly." The most shocking accusation was the final one. Max and Marty were accused of "touching the forenamed player aggressively and inappropriately."

"What's that last part mean?" Marty asked Max. "Touching him inappropriately?"

Max read on. "It means in a game you pushed him hard from behind while he was sitting on the bench. Mr. Winters calls that assault."

Marty would have laughed if the charge hadn't been so serious. "I tapped him on the back," he recalled. "Told him to be ready to jump on the ice. He was daydreaming."

Max cleared his throat and read on. "The lawyer says that I assaulted him as well. Mr. Winters saw me attempt to strangle his son after a game."

"That was after he scored the winning goal," Marty exclaimed, stunned by the charge. "You threw your arm around his neck to congratulate him."

"I know," said Max. "But apparently Mr. Winters didn't see it that way. Now he's hauling us into court. We have to appear before Judge Gaul next Friday."

"This is scary," Marty said. "What if we're convicted? We could go to jail. And all because a father thinks we're stopping his son from becoming an NHLer."

"I'm not so sure Danny even aspires to an NHL career," said Max. "I don't think he knows what he wants. Who does at his age?"

"No, but his father wants it for him," Marty said glumly. He sighed. "When we volunteered to take this coaching job, we didn't anticipate all the headaches it would bring."

Judge Gaul heard testimony in the case on Friday afternoon after school. It was the last case of his day.

He heard the lawyer for Mr. Winters give the background of the case, and then Mr. Winters took the stand. His wife and his son Danny listened intently from a nearby bench.

The Mitchells, dressed in their Sunday suits, sat together on chairs at the front of the courtroom. Their parents were seated behind them, in the first row of benches.

Mr. Winters delivered a scathing attack on the Mitchells, calling them callous and irresponsible in their treatment of his son. "Danny is a shattered young boy. His dreams of playing in the NHL have been destroyed," he claimed. He pointed a finger at Max and Marty. "My son may need psychiatric care for months because of the trauma he suffered at the hands of these so-called coaches." He turned to Judge Gaul. "Look at my son, Your Honour! He's distraught. Humiliated. He has been robbed of his chance to play hockey. He was beloved by his teammates."

There was shuffling at the back of the courtroom. Led by Tim Robbins, a number of River Rats quietly entered the room and sat down.

"My biggest concern, Your Honour," Mr. Winters continued, "was the shocking display of inappropriate behaviour by the Mitchell brothers. By that I mean the touching and shoving of Danny by his coaches, which, in my opinion, should be construed as assault. For all of the reasons I've stated, and for all of the suffering inflicted on my son and my family by the Mitchells, I look for the court to award me the sum of 100 thousand dollars at the minimum."

"Who speaks for the defendants?" asked the judge.

"I do, Your Honour," Max said.

After being sworn to tell the truth and only the truth, Max was asked to tell his side of the story.

Clearly and concisely, he described how and why he and Marty had decided to drop Danny Winters from the team. He said that they quite liked Danny but his failing grades at school had cost him his position on the team.

"What about the rather serious charge that you and your brother assaulted Danny inappropriately?" Judge Gaul asked. "How do you respond?"

"We're astonished by the charge, Your Honour," Max replied. "My brother poked Danny on the shoulder to get his attention, to get him out on the ice. He wasn't focused on the game. And I admit to throwing my arm around his neck after he scored the winning goal. If that's assault, then I suppose I'm guilty."

"What's your opinion of Mr. Winters as a hockey father?" the judge asked Max.

Max hesitated. He looked at Mr. Winters. Then he said, "Your Honour, Mr. Winters hopes Danny will play in the NHL one day. But at this stage of his hockey career, Danny is just an average player. Danny seems to know that, but his father believes he's an all-star. His father has been a distraction, refusing to leave the dressing room when we have our meetings before games. And I understand he's been quite vocal in his criticism of my brother and me behind our backs.

"Frankly, sir, I feel sorry for sons who have fathers like Mr. Winters. And I'm astonished that he would take legal action against us, making ridiculous and totally untrue charges."

A smattering of applause from the River Rats prompted the judge to raise his hand and call, "Silence in the court."

"You may sit down, Mr. Mitchell," he said to Max.

He motioned for Danny Winters to come forward. In a kindly voice, he asked Danny if he thought he had been mistreated by the Mitchell brothers.

"Not really."

"Did either of them ever touch you inappropriately?"

"No. Marty poked me on the shoulder once when I was daydreaming."

"What were you daydreaming about?"

"Music. I was thinking about how I liked music a lot better than hockey. I wanted to get home and play my guitar."

"Do you feel your life has been ruined by your dismissal from the River Rats? Are you devastated and humiliated by what happened?"

"No. Getting dropped from the team doesn't bother me. I've got my music and I'll have more time to play in the school band." He smiled. "Nobody gets bodychecked in the band. Or gets cracked over the head. Unless the drum major clips him with a drum stick."

A wave of laughter rolled through the court-room.

"Thank you, Danny. Now I'm going to ask you to leave the room. I have some things I want to say to your father—and your mother—and I'd rather you not hear them."

"Sure." Danny slipped out of the room. He tossed a friendly wave to the River Rats as he made his exit.

The judge shuffled some papers on his desk, and then stared solemnly at the small number of people in his courtroom.

"It's been a long day in court," Judge Gaul sighed. "I've been called upon to settle several serious disputes. But to end my workday with a case of this nature, a case this frivolous, this...unnecessary, is anger-provoking and disturbing to say the least.

"Mr. Winters, your demand for the sum of 100 thousand dollars for damages to your precious son's confidence and self-esteem is outrageous. I played on teams when I was young. And I have coached teams. I find no fault with the actions of the Mitchell brothers but I am appalled that you, sir, as a parent, would subject your family— especially your son—to this course of action.

"You would be well advised to deal with your son's emotional problems, if indeed they exist. It could well be that his poor performance in the classroom is caused by pressure applied by you, his father, to excel in hockey. It disturbs me that you seem to harbour unrealistic expectations for your son in hockey. And it appears to me that he is happy to be free of the game and the pressure. Now he can focus on becoming a musician.

"I am no psychiatrist, Mr. Winters, but perhaps you should go see one. And talk to Danny's teachers. But I caution you not to blame two dedicated volunteer coaches for your son's problems.

"All charges against the Mitchell brothers are dismissed. And the court costs for this action will be the responsibility of Mr. Winters."

Judge Gaul glared at Mr. Winters. "My dear sir," he growled, "I strongly advise you to think twice before ever entering my courtroom again with such unfounded accusations."

Then he glared at Mr. Winter's lawyer. "And you, sir, should have advised your client to avoid my courtroom at all costs."

He slammed his gavel on the desk in anger, stood and left the bench. But not before giving a thumbs up to the River Rats and calling out, "Good luck, boys!"

CHAPTER 11

CONFRONTING THE COBRAS

One morning on their way to school, the Mitchell brothers stopped by the rink on the river.

"I think I left one of my hockey sticks in one of the fish huts," Max said to Marty. "I was going to tape it this morning but I couldn't find it at home."

Marty shrugged. "We haven't had time to put a lock on the door, but it should be there. Nobody ever locks their doors in Indian River."

But when they made their way over the snow-banks to the river's edge, they recoiled in shock.

"Look at the ice!" Max cried out. "Something's wrong with it! It's brown!"

They rushed onto the ice and found themselves standing in a mix of sand and gravel.

"I can't believe it!" Marty cried, sliding his foot over the surface. "Our rink is ruined. Somebody's thrown gunk all over it. And it looks like they played hockey before they dumped on it. There are skate marks under the gunk."

Max was equally aghast. "Look at the tire tracks, Marty," he said, pointing. "This is awful. Someone drove in here and dumped a load of sand and gravel all over our ice. We can never practice on this."

Marty pulled his brother by the elbow and pointed toward the fish huts.

"Look at the fish huts, Max! The doors to our dressing rooms are wide open. Somebody's been poking around in there. Let's go see."

They ran to the nearest hut and gasped. The door had been pulled from its hinges and the interior of the hut had been vandalized. The players' benches had been overturned and broken. The potbelly stove lay on its side. There were holes in the roof and in the walls.

"Oh, no!" Marty wailed. "Someone's destroyed it!"

"Quick! Check the other hut," Max said as he rushed out the door.

The second hut was similarly ransacked. Broken door, broken benches, upturned stove.

"Somebody's been through these huts with an axe," Max howled. "Some rotten vandals!"

"They've destroyed everything," Marty said angrily. "After all the hard work folks did. The stinkers! But who would do such a thing?"

"It may have been some of the older kids who skate on the river," Max suggested. "There's a gang downriver called the Cobras. They may have been jealous of our team having a nice little rink—with lights and all."

"Maybe," Marty said. "But that would surprise me. We know most of those kids. They're a tough bunch but it's hard to believe they would do this to us." He sighed and looked around. "What a mess! Now what are we going to do?"

Max shrugged. "First thing we've got to do is tell Mom and Dad. I'll call them from school. Mom can phone the parents and tell them today's practice has been cancelled."

"Okay. Let's get going. We don't want to be late. We'll come back here after school—in case some of the kids don't get Mom's message and show up."

Marty stopped suddenly and pulled Max by the sleeve. "By the way, where's your hockey stick?"

Max looked grim. "It's not here," he said. "Somebody stole it."

"Your brand new stick! You paid a buck for it. I hope you had your name on it."

"Yep, I did," was the reply. "I put my name on it yesterday. With a black marker. But I doubt I'll ever see that stick again."

After school, accompanied by Trudy, the boys returned to the rink. It was Marty who noticed something they'd missed that morning.

"Look!" he said. "There's a broken stick somebody stuck in a snowbank. Maybe that'll give us a clue to who did this."

They pulled the stick from the snow and brushed it off. There was a name in black ink on the upper part of the shaft. DEADMARSH.

"That's Dutchie Deadmarsh's stick," Marty gasped. "He's the biggest, meanest guy in town. Isn't he the leader of the Cobras?"

Max looked grim. "You're right. They're tough guys, the Cobras. They play games of shinny farther down the river on weekends. They're a wild bunch—on and off the ice.

"Deadmarsh has been in trouble with the law a couple of times," Trudy added.

"What are we going to do, Max?" Marty groaned. "It looks like the Cobras used our rink for at least one of their games, then ruined it."

"Let's go," Max said.

"Go where?"

"We'll go see them. We can't let them get away with this."

"You sure, Max? Shouldn't we talk to the police first? Or Dad? The Cobras will likely beat us up."

Max held up the broken stick. "This is the only proof we have that the Cobras were here. It's not enough. No, we'll go have a talk with Dutchie Deadmarsh."

Max, Marty and Trudy skated down the river. Soon they heard the whoops and howls of young men at play.

They rounded a bend in the river, and there they were—the Cobras. At least ten of them, playing a scrambly game of shinny.

Marty slowed his pace. "They're big guys, Max. And older than us. Be careful what you say."

"You two stay back. Let me handle this," Max cautioned Marty and Trudy. "But we can't chicken out. We've got to have it out with them."

Max plunged ahead, and skated right into the middle of the scrimmage.

"Hey, you!" someone shouted. "Get the heck off the ice! No outsiders allowed!"

Max ignored the command. He trapped the loose puck with his skate and kicked it toward the shore.

"That does it," one of the Cobras bellowed. He flashed across the ice and would have barrelled into Max if he hadn't stepped nimbly aside. The irate Cobra flew past, tripped and skidded across the ice on his backside. The other players laughed.

"Hey, Alfie!" one of them roared sarcastically. "That's showin' him, you goofball."

Another Cobra, the biggest of the lot, dropped his stick, charged forward and shoved Max in the chest, almost toppling him. But Max anticipated the attack, dug in with his skates and pushed back.

"Hey, Deadmarsh," Max grunted, as he dodged a punch to the head. "I want to talk to you. You and your gang ruined our hockey rink."

"We'll talk later, punk," Deadmarsh growled. "First I'll teach you not to barge in where you're not welcome."

He lashed out with another punch that landed on Max's shoulder. Max choked back a howl of pain and felt a jolt of anger erupt inside him.

Deadmarsh was wearing a long red scarf knotted around his neck. Max reached out and gripped it with his left hand, pulling Deadmarsh toward him. At the same time, he swung his right hand into Deadmarsh's face. Once, twice, three times.

Blood spurted from Deadmarsh's large nose. He howled with rage and used his superior weight to wrestle Max to the ice. Brute strength gave him an advantage over Max, who was lighter but more agile. Max squirmed and twisted and applied pressure to the knot in the scarf until Deadmarsh began to gasp for air. Suddenly, Max released the scarf, gripped his opponent by the shoulders and flipped him over on his back. Deadmarsh hit the ice with a thud. Max was on top of him, applying a headlock with one arm, gripping the knotted scarf with the other.

Deadmarsh was pinned to the ice, and his breathing was ragged. Like most bullies, he was quick to surrender, to give up when things didn't go his way. The kid he was wrestling was like a bulldog.

"Hey! That's enough," he muttered, realizing he could not break the hold Max was applying, or win the battle.

"Let's talk," Max muttered in his ear. "But keep your goons away when I let you up. Promise!"

"Sure, I promise. I'll talk. Just let me up."

Max released his hold and both young men scrambled to their feet. Deadmarsh reached for some snow on the ice and applied it to his bloody nose.

Some of the other Cobras moved forward menacingly, but Deadmarsh held them back with an upraised arm.

"Stay back. It's over," he said. "This kid pinned me good." He chuckled. "And I think he broke my nose. He's a scrapper."

"Dutchie, you look better with your nose all bent like a pretzel," one of the Cobras said, showing no sympathy.

Dutchie turned to the Mitchells. "Look, I'll admit it. We used your two-bit rink for a hockey scrimmage. What's the big deal?"

Max was still angry. "The big deal is that you destroyed our ice when you were finished playing. With gravel and pebbles. And you wrecked our dressing room. And someone stole my best stick."

Dutchie's eyebrows shot up in surprise.

"We didn't do that," he said. "Why would we ruin your ice and smash up your clubhouse?"

"That's why I'm here," Max replied. "To ask you why."

Deadmarsh turned to his followers. "Did we play hockey on their stupid rink, guys?"

Several voices answered, "Yes."

"And did we steal any sticks and throw gravel around?"

A louder chorus answered, "No!"

Max looked into their faces. He guessed they were telling the truth.

"Okay, I believe you," he said. "But I want you to know we worked hard to build that rink. It's for little kids, not grownups. My brother and I would appreciate it if you'd stay off it." He waved an arm and looked around. "You've got the whole river to skate on. Okay?"

"Sure. What do we care what you do?" said one of the Cobras.

"Now we've got to go back and figure out how to clean up the mess someone left on our rink," Marty added. He couldn't resist getting in a word or two.

Max, Marty and Trudy turned their backs and began to skate away.

But Marty noticed Dutchie Deadmarsh skating up behind Max and called out a warning. "Max!

Look out!"

Max whirled and raised his fists, anticipating a sneak attack.

"Hey, put 'em away," Deadmarsh said with a laugh. He threw his arms up in mock surrender and Max noticed that both of his eyes had begun to blacken. "I just want to send you off with three little words."

"Oh, yeah?" Max asked suspiciously. "What are they?"

"Good luck, pal."

CHAPTER 12

A ROUGH GAME ON THE ROAD

That night, Max and Marty sat around the kitchen table and talked with their parents about the vandalism.

"What a shame," Amy Mitchell said. "The boys loved playing on that outdoor rink. Some of the parents were really upset when I told them what happened."

"I called the police," their father said. "The sergeant on duty promised to drive over to the rink and see if he could find any clues left around. Called back to say he didn't find a thing. He figures some older kids did the damage—just for the heck of it."

"But what should we do now, Dad?" Marty asked. "We could start all over and make a new rink. Or we could spend the next few days trying to shovel the sand and gravel off the one that was vandalized."

"That's a lot of work," their mother said. "And who's to say the vandals won't come back and do some more damage."

"What about finding a new practice rink away from the river?" Max suggested. "Somewhere secluded, a place nobody knows about."

"You mean like a backyard rink?" Marty asked. "There are lots in town but they're mostly small. Not big enough for a peewee team to practice on."

Max snapped his fingers and jumped up and ran from the room.

"I just thought of something," he said. "I've got to make a phone call."

In five minutes he was back, a grin on his face.

"It's all settled," he announced. "We've got a new practice rink, nets and all. We've even got a string of lights over it. And a big barn for a dressing room."

"That's great news!" Marty leaped up and high-fived his brother. "Amazing! Where is it?"

"Near Turtle Creek. On Mr. Stanowski's farm pond. You saw it, Marty. On the day we went skiing. It's perfect for us. The ice is at least a foot thick by now."

At first Marty was enthused. Then he said, "But it's quite a drive out there. How'll we get the fellows back and forth?"

Max looked at his father. "Dad, if you can lend us the car a couple of times a week, we can drive three or four of the boys. You can drive the truck to work. And three players who live out that way won't need a drive—Nicole and the Stanowski twins."

"What about the rest of them?" Marty asked. "They can all squeeze into another car—if it's big enough. Let's see... Who drives a big car in Indian River?"

Max began to chuckle.

"Tell us, brother," Marty said. "You've already thought of that, haven't you?"

"I made a second phone call a minute ago. I got lucky. Miss Fallis showed up at one of our games—and she's got the biggest car in Indian River. Her father was a funeral director. He died last year and left it to her in his will."

"You mean it's a hearse?"

"Right. At least it used to be. She's embarrassed to drive it and was going to sell it. When I told her we needed help getting players to Mr. Stanowski's farm, she said she'd do it. Miss Fallis has an assistant at the library who can take over when she has to leave early."

Marty laughed knowingly. "I'll bet she volunteered in a hurry after you mentioned Mr. Stanowski."

Amy Mitchell smiled and asked, "You mean there's something..."

"Mom, it's pretty plain to us," Max said. "We think Miss Fallis has...you know...a thing for Mr. Stanowski."

"Well, blow me down," said their father, sounding like Popeye. "Miss Fallis? The shy little librarian with no makeup and her hair in a bun? Who'd have thunk it?"

The River Rats enjoyed their new rink almost as much as the old one. For the next couple of weeks, they commuted twice a week to Mr. Stanowski's farm pond. Mr. Stanowski kept the ice free of snow and filled cracks in the surface with water.

He had offered part of his big barn as a dressing room, then thought better of it.

"Use the kitchen, boys," he said. "It's warm and roomy. Miss Fallis and I will clean up after you."

"And I'll prepare some hot soup for you to eat after the practices," Miss Fallis promised. "And bake some cookies, too, if Mr. Stanowski will let me use his oven."

Mr Stanowski beamed and said, "Be my guest, Miss Fallis. But please call me Silas."

"I will," she promised, "if you'll call me Stella."

Max and Marty noticed that the twins, who were lacing up their skates, stopped to exchange a secretive smile.

Miss Fallis turned out to be a popular chauffeur when she drove them to practice.

"She's so smart and entertaining," Squirt told Max and Marty one day. "She tells great stories to the fellows and she's always urging us to read more and learn more. She wants us all to think about going to college some day. And those cookies she bakes! Mmmm, mmmm."

In mid-February, the River Rats were invited to play an exhibition game in Turtle Creek—on an open-air rink similar to the one on the Stanowski farm. Mr. Falzone extended the invitation by phone.

"A fellow called me the other day. He's put together a pretty fair team out this way. They've run up some big scores against teams from surrounding towns. Now he'd like to test his boys against the River Rats. He'd like to play you fellows on Sunday afternoon. Two o'clock."

"Sounds good," Max said. "The River Rats would enjoy playing a road game. You set things up, Mr. Falzone. We'll be there."

The River Rats were excited about the exhibition game. "Maybe we could travel there by train," Tim Robbins suggested. "You know, like the big leaguers do.

Max laughed. "Tim, you know the train doesn't stop in a tiny place like Turtle Creek," he said. "But I have another idea. How about we go by horse-drawn sled? Have any of you been on a sleigh ride?"

Only one or two of the players had experienced

the joy of a winter sleigh ride, and Max's proposal was endorsed unanimously.

They started out on Sunday morning after church. The players wore heavy jackets over their hockey uniforms. Hats, mitts, scarves and earmuffs were part of every player's wardrobe. A number of girls in school heard about the junket and pleaded to be included. They called themselves the River Rats Fan Club and they showed up with sandwiches, cookies, cake and soft drinks to show their appreciation.

One of the girls had a crush on Marty. She offered him a cookie, a rock hard crispy disc that had been scorched in the oven. "I bake two things really well," she said proudly. "Brownies and chocolate chip cookies."

"Great," Marty replied. "Which one is this?"

Harry and Amy Mitchell acted as chaperones and led the happy group in a singsong that lasted all the way to Turtle Creek. There they were met by the Falzone and Stanowski families who climbed on board the sleigh.

"Is Joe coming?" Max asked Mr. Stanowski.

"No, he's in his room studying."

"Where to now?" the driver shouted.

"Just over that hill on the far side of town," Mr. Falzone directed. "Just past the gravel pit. The other team is waiting for us. They call themselves the Turtle Creek Terrors."

"Turn left here," he called out, and the horses swung obediently down a farmer's lane.

A name on the gate caught Max and Marty's eye. Together they shouted, "Oh, no!"

"What is it?" their mother asked.

"This is Whizzer Wilson's place," Max moaned. "The sign said Wilson Sand and Gravel. I never thought..."

"How could this happen?" Marty moaned. "We've been suckered."

Mr. Falzone, noting their distress, tried to explain, "Mr. Wilson sounded nice enough on the phone," he said. "I didn't know you knew each other or that you disliked each other. I'm so sorry I made these arrangements. Look! Let's turn around. Let's just go back."

"No, we can't do that," Mr. Mitchell ruled. "The boys have had such a good time so far. And they've been looking forward to this game. We have to go through with it. Maybe Wilson has changed his tune since we saw him last."

"And maybe his players will be good sports," said Marty. "After all, it's just an exhibition game."

The game had been well publicized in Turtle Creek and a number of cars, trucks and sleighs lined the long driveway. At least 100 people stood around the ice surface, and a number of children had climbed nearby trees to get a better view of the action on the ice.

During the warm-up, Max and Marty noticed a familiar figure circulating through the crowd, holding out his hat, taking up a collection.

"That's Whizzer Wilson," Max snorted. "I can't believe he's making money on this game."

"And I can't believe some of his players aren't older than our boys. Too old for peewee hockey. They're big, tough farm boys. Much bigger than the River Rats. I don't like the looks of this. We're in for a battle."

"Oh, no," Marty wailed. "Look who just stepped on the ice for the Terrors. It's Wally Wilson."

Holding a stick with a shaft as thick as a tree branch, Wally Wilson skated into the warm-up and boldly moved close to Tim Robbins.

"So we meet again," he growled, lifting his stick menacingly. "Now it's payback time for the way you fellows treated me."

"We didn't do anything to you," Tim said icily. "You quit on us! You thought you knew more than our coaches. Why are you such a troublemaker—why not just play hockey?"

"I will," Wally countered. "And I may use your head for a puck."

Tim warned his teammates to keep a close eye on Wally. "He hits anything that moves," he said.

Squirt Bragan drew a laugh when he chirped, "That's okay. I won't move."

From the opening faceoff, Wilson and the

Terrors stepped into their smaller opponents. A number of crushing checks left the River Rats dazed and bewildered. And the referee, a Turtle Creek resident who bought gravel from Whizzer Wilson, just laughed when Max and Marty cried out for penalties.

The Terrors quickly pulled into a 3–0 lead.

By the end of the first period, the River Rats felt like they'd been pulled through the wringer of a washing machine and held up to dry. They were bruised and battered and welcomed the first intermission. They rested on blankets on their sleigh. "Those guys are mean," gasped Tim Robbins. "What did we do to deserve this?"

A local farmer overheard and chuckled. He said, "That'll teach you to badmouth our good neighbour."

"What neighbour? What do you mean?" Tim asked. "We didn't badmouth anyone."

"Liar," snarled the man. "We heard all about it from Whizzer. How you called him names. How you little squirts called him a rotten coach. And how the Mitchell boys stole his team and ganged up on him and tried to beat him up. Now you pups will get a taste of your own medicine."

"But that's preposterous!" Max exclaimed. "Sure, some of the boys called him a rotten coach. Maybe he is one. But my brother and I never beat him up. He threatened our dad..."

"Bull!" the man barked angrily. "Whizzer told us what happened. Now you've fallen into his trap." He waved an arm at the sizeable crowd. "These folks are Whizzer's friends and relatives. They're here to see you River Rats take a beating on the ice. And after the game, they can watch as Whizzer's pals give you and your dad a good licking."

"Leave my dad out of this," Max said hotly. "We'll deal with Whizzer, but why pick on my father?"

"Because he wrote a nasty column in that rag he calls a paper. All about Whizzer's temper. How he's a goon on the ice. We didn't take kindly to that here in Turtle Creek. I can't wait to see you Mitchells get what's coming to you." The man moved away, laughing like a movie villain who thinks he has the upper hand.

Just then Mr. Mitchell appeared. He'd gone for water for the players but came back empty-handed.

"There's a well but I couldn't get close to it," he said. "Some fellows told me to get in line but the line never seemed to move. And when it did they pushed me to the back of it." He turned to the players. "Sorry, boys, I tried. I know how thirsty you must be. We should have brought our own water. Nobody thought..."

Trudy turned to her father, who had driven to the game, arriving late. "Dad, lend me your car

119

keys. I'll get the boys some water. And I'll get them something else, too." She took the keys and hurried off down the lane.

Max and Marty took their father aside and told him what they'd heard—how Whizzer and his thugs planned to beat them up. "We don't know what to do," Max said. "We don't want our kids getting hurt."

"Let's hope he's just trying to frighten us," said Mr. Mitchell. "Perhaps we should stop the game right now. Perhaps we should just go on home."

"Dad, look down the lane. Someone has closed the gate. And some tough-looking guys are guarding it. I think we're trapped."

"I can't believe this is happening," Harry Mitchell said, his temper rising. "I'm going to find Whizzer. I'll demand an explanation."

He was back in five minutes, looking dejected.

"What happened, Dad?" Marty asked. "Did you find him?"

"He laughed in my face," their father said. "Told me I was imagining things. I think he's lost his mind."

"Can we leave?" Marty asked. "Can we get out of here?"

"I'm afraid not, boys. He insisted the game go on—or else. He did say he'd have his team ease up on our boys—but with some conditions."

"What are they?"

"That we play the game to a finish. And that I write an apology to Whizzer in the paper. I told him we'd stay but I'd have to think about the apology. I'm not going to, of course. And there was one more thing."

"Tell us."

"He said he wants us to stay around and meet his buddies—the Slugg brothers."

"I've heard of them," Max said. "They're tough as nails."

"That's what worries me," their father said. "He said the Sluggs can't wait to meet you and Marty."

CHAPTER 13

TRAPPED

The referee barked at the players, ordering them back on the ice. But Max held the River Rats back. He had some things to say to them.

"We can quit right now," he told them. "This game is far rougher than it should be. Whizzer and Wally are obviously out for revenge. They want to make you boys suffer. But Marty and I don't want anyone getting hurt. Most of your parents stayed home today, but if they were here they might demand that you quit. We're pretty much on our own here. What do you say?"

Tim stepped forward. "We shouldn't quit," he said. "Sure they're big and they're tough. Hockey isn't for sissies—or quitters. And the River Rats are neither. Come on, fellows, let's get back on the ice. Let's beat those...those...manure spreaders."

Tim's little speech worked wonders. The River Rats came out aggressively in the second period. Bodychecks that had rocked them earlier failed to land. Why? Because the visitors played heads-up hockey and sidestepped most of the bodyslams. And when some of the smaller players were knocked off their feet, defencemen Chubby Thomas and Roddy Barnaby barrelled into the bullies who started the rough stuff.

Wally Wilson and his mates grew frustrated and lunged recklessly at the faster River Rats. The Terrors chased them around the ice and ignored the object of the game—to score goals.

The Terrors became infuriated when Tim Robbins snared a loose puck and raced in to beat the Turtle Creek goaltender with a nifty deke and a shot to the corner. They spent the rest of the period chasing after Tim like a posse chasing a cattle thief. And each time they appeared to have him trapped, he sprinted free.

During the second intermission, Trudy appeared with some bottles of water, which the River Rats gulped greedily.

"I had to go all the way back to the Stanowski house to get it," she explained. "Sorry it took so long. But I had to use the phone while I was there."

"Who'd you call?" Marty asked.

"Never mind," she said, giving him a strange look.

The third period began, and the Terrors continued to hound the River Rats. During a faceoff, Wally Wilson sidled up to Squirt Bragan and tried to intimidate him.

"Why, you sawed off little so-and-so," he snarled. "What are you going to be when you grow up?"

"Something you'll never be," Bragan fired back. "A goal scorer!"

The referee was still laughing at Bragan's quip when he dropped the puck.

It was at this point that the River Rats rallied behind Tim Robbins, their leader, and began to strike back when challenged. Any fear of their opponents disappeared when Tim and Wally Wilson clashed at centre ice.

Tim went down heavily after Wilson stuck his heavy stick between Tim's legs and twisted it, throwing Tim to the ice.

Tim lost his temper momentarily. He jumped up and yanked Wally's stick from his hands. He stepped on the blade, snapping it from the shaft.

"Play with that!" Tim snapped, shoving the stick into Wally's hands.

Wally was so surprised that he did attempt to play with the stick, swiping futilely at the puck until the referee blew his whistle.

"Two minutes," he barked. "Playing with a broken stick."

It was the only penalty he handed to the Terrors in the hockey game. But while Wilson was off, the River Rats barged in and scored their second goal,

Tim collecting it with a shot from ten feet out.

The Terrors were able to cling to their lead until the final minute of play. With time running out, anxious to score an insurance goal, Wally fumbled a pass inside the River Rats zone. Tim snapped up the loose puck, raced down the ice and flipped a scoring shot over the goalie's shoulder. Tie game, and a hat trick for Tim!

Wally Wilson, exasperated over his miscue, had chased Tim furiously but couldn't catch up. He stumbled when he reached the end boards, and with no screen to save him, flew headlong into the snowbank surrounding the rink. He was buried in snow. Gales of laughter erupted from the spectators. Two of them hurried over to grab Wally by the skates and haul him out. Bits of snow flew from his nose and mouth as he came free, gasping and snorting.

Embarrassed, he hurried off the ice. "That's it for me," he told his Uncle Whizzer as he left.

"You're nothing but a quitter," Whizzer told him angrily. "Go get dressed."

With only seconds left to play, and the faceoff at centre ice, Whizzer cupped his hands and bellowed at his weary players.

"Yer all quitters! I'm ashamed of you!"

The Terrors were startled at this outburst and turned to stare in surprise. But Tim Robbins was not distracted or surprised. He'd heard Whizzer's outbursts before. While the Terrors gaped, he took the puck, skated right through them and popped in the winning goal. Just like that, easy as pie.

The River Rats won the game 4–3.

Max and Marty leaped up on the planks that served as the visiting team's bench and whooped for joy.

"Great game, guys! Great game!" Max hollered.

"Way to go, River Rats!" Marty shouted. He took another leap in the air, came down hard on the plank and cracked it in two. He held on to Max and laughed out loud.

"Listen, Marty," Max said. "The fans are applauding the River Rats. I thought they were all friends of Whizzer—many of them are parents of the Terrors."

"Sure they are. But they know a gritty performance when they see it, and they saw a terrific comeback today. Now let's get the boys back on the sleigh and get out of here."

But a dozen young men blocked their path to the gate. The sleigh skidded to a halt. Two broad-shouldered young men stepped forward. They were a rough looking pair, bold and insolent. They were dressed in stained parkas and wore heavy work boots.

"We're the Slugg brothers," one of them announced. "You may have heard of us. I'm Bart. This here's Buster."

Buster Slugg grinned, exposing crooked teeth stained from chewing tobacco. He pointed at Max and Marty.

"We want to see you two," he declared. "How be we step in behind the barn? Won't take but a minute or two."

CHAPTER 14

SAVED FROM A BEATING

Mr. Mitchell acted swiftly. He ordered the driver of the sleigh to change direction and take the sleigh across the open field and through another exit. The driver protested, saying, "Sir, you and your boys may need help," but Mr. Mitchell barked at him, "Get the River Rats home to Indian River. Their safety is all-important. We'll catch a ride back with Trudy and Mr. Reeves. Now move!"

The sleigh bells jingled as the driver pulled on the reins, changing course. The horses bolted off across the field, snow flying from their hooves.

Mr. Mitchell stepped forward and confronted the Sluggs. "You leave my sons alone," he hissed. "I'll have you charged if you touch them."

The brothers laughed. One of them made a motion with his head, and several of his cronies jumped in and grabbed Mr. Mitchell by the arms. He was immobilized. Mr. Stanowski, Mr. Reeves and Mr. Falzone received similar treatment when they came to Harry Mitchell's aid.

Max and Marty rushed forward to assist their father, but other young men swiftly blocked their path. They too were handled roughly by members of the Slugg gang.

"Take the Mitchell kids in behind the barn!" the Sluggs ordered. "They won't look so pretty when they come out."

The Mitchell brothers were dragged through the snow toward the barn. They could not break free of their burly captors.

Whizzer Wilson stood some distance away, a smile on his face. "You're responsible for this, Wilson!" Max shouted as they passed him. "You set us up!"

Wilson chuckled. "I don't know what you're talking about, Mitchell. Why, I hardly know the Sluggs. But whatever you did to make them mad, it looks like you're about to pay for it."

When a number of curious spectators and a few young children tried to follow the procession to the barn, Wilson shooed them away. "Don't go back there," he warned them. "Go home! This is a private matter."

The barn loomed up and the Mitchell brothers were dragged in behind it. Max whispered to Marty, "We're going to take a beating, but let's try to surprise the Sluggs. You follow my lead."

The brothers were pushed up against the barn, their backs to the wall. Only then were their arms released. Max glanced around, looking for anything he could use as a weapon. Next to where he stood lay a pile of loose boards, half buried in the snow. "Remember, follow my lead," he muttered to Marty.

The Sluggs took off their parkas and dropped them in the snow. They flexed their muscles and advanced on the Mitchells, savouring the moment. The other thugs stood back, forming a semicircle.

"We almost hate to do this to you," Bart, the older brother, sneered. "It's going to be such a mismatch. You don't look nearly tough enough to give us a good fight."

"But someone was willing to pay us a nice fee to teach you a lesson," Buster chipped in. "You boys shouldn't go around antagonizing people. We don't have to tell you who we mean."

"We know who you mean," Max said bitterly.

"Maybe you fellows want to take a moment to say your prayers," Bart laughed. "Not that it'll do you any good."

"Sure, maybe we'll do that," Max answered coldly. He dropped to his knees. Marty followed his lead and dropped down next to him. They bowed their heads.

The young toughs laughed aloud. "Scared little rabbits, ain't they?" Bart Slugg chuckled. "They're praying when they ain't got a prayer."

But Max and Marty weren't kneeling to pray. They came up off their knees with weapons in their hands—four-foot-long chunks of lumber snatched from the scrap pile at their feet. And they came up swinging.

The Sluggs leaped back in surprise when they saw the Mitchells were no longer defenceless. But too late.

Thwack!

Max struck the elder Slugg across the shins with a well-aimed blow. The bully's scream of pain and outrage filled the air. Bart Slugg flew backwards, sending two of his supporters sprawling.

Buster Slugg turned to look. He was caught off guard and gaped, stunned by the attack.

Crack!

Buster Slugg took the full force of Marty's blows, one to his knees and, when he spun around, a second to his backside. He howled like a hungry dog and tumbled face first into the snow. Fuming and snarling, the Slugg brothers lunged to their feet, clutching their knees, furious at being outsmarted and unprepared.

"Let's get 'em, Marty!" Max yelled.

Bart Slugg was wiping snow from his face when Max staggered him with a right-handed punch that opened up a cut on his cheek. He howled again.

Marty threw three short punches—bap-bap-bap—into the face of Buster Slugg, who slipped in the snow and fell down for the second time.

But the Mitchell brothers' sudden attack was cut short. They were gang-tackled and hurled to the ground, pinned under the weight of half a dozen men.

Slowly, Bart and Buster Slugg advanced on them.

"Drag them to their feet," Bart Slugg ordered. "I want these two punks to see the punches coming."

Max and Marty were pulled upright and thrust roughly up against the barn wall. The weapons that had served them well were kicked aside, and their arms were pinned to their sides by two heavily muscled youths.

Bart and Buster, their faces bruised and bloodied, spat into the palms of their hands. They clenched their fists and raised them high. Max and Marty turned their heads and closed their eyes, bracing themselves for a pounding they couldn't avoid.

"Stop right there!" a sharp voice commanded. "Get away from those boys!"

Bart and Buster dropped their fists and swung around in surprise. Max and Marty opened their eyes and whooped for joy. They would suffer no beating on this day. For the Slugg gang was now out-numbered by a group of larger, stronger, more dangerous-looking fellows, men everybody recognized, men with a reputation for toughness that far exceeded their own.

The Cobras had arrived—and just in time.

Led by Dutchie Deadmarsh, they advanced on the Sluggs and some of the latter group began to scatter. The Sluggs feared Dutchie, and Dutchie knew it. He slapped Bart Slugg across the face—hard. Then he took Buster Slugg by the shoulder, pinned him up against the barn and slapped him, too.

"Don't you ever touch the Mitchell boys, or you'll live to regret it!" Dutchie threatened through clenched teeth. "Don't ever mess with friends of the Cobras!"

He spun both Sluggs around and kicked each in the behind—hard. "You stiffs get out of here!" he barked. "Move it!"

In seconds the bullies had vanished and the Mitchell brothers were thanking their rescuers.

"It was Trudy, wasn't it?" Max said to Dutchie after expelling a sigh of relief. His heart was still pounding, but he was breathing almost normally again. "She called you to come and help us, I'll bet."

"Good guess, partner," Dutchie said, slapping Max on the shoulder. "Course it took me awhile to round up my buddies. But the Cobras are always ready for a bit of excitement."

"It's a good thing they are," Marty interjected, wiping his sweaty brow. "Another minute and our faces would look like Mom's meat loaf."

The Cobras laughed.

Just then Mr. Mitchell came charging around the end of the barn, followed by Mr. Reeves, Mr. Falzone and Mr. Stanowski.

"Those birds who were holding us dropped us like hot potatoes," Mr. Mitchell gasped. "They saw the Sluggs come tearing out from behind the barn and they fled with the rest of them. Something frightened them."

He looked at the Cobras in surprise. Then he smiled. "Must have been you fellows."

Max laughed. "You've got that right, Dad. Meet our friends, the Cobras. They just saved our bacon. They came out from Indian River on their motorcycles."

"Yep," said Dutchie. "We stopped a half mile down the road, then slogged through the gravel pit, up to our knees in snow. We crept through those evergreens on the far side of the barn. Caught the Sluggs by surprise. By golly, it was worth it to see those dummies look so stunned. And to save your boys from being pounded on by those bullies."

CHAPTER 15

MR. MITCHELL SPEAKS OUT

By mid-week, Mr. Mitchell had finished his editorial, and it created quite a stir when it was printed in the *Review*

Where Is Minor Hockey Headed?

Minor hockey is supposed to be fun for the kids in Indian River, the young guys—and a few girls— who play organized hockey and enjoy it. But the game, we were surprised to learn, is inundated with problems, most of them created by over- zealous coaches and parents.

One team in our community—a team of pee- wees—has been forced to deal with a surprising number of disturbing incidents this winter. And there's still a month left in the season.

Our research has revealed the following:

1. A coach screamed at players and officials, sav- agely ripping into young men who were trying their best to play the game and regulate it. The coach retired from hockey rather than face a suspension or banishment from the game. According to his players and other witnesses, the coach often used profane and abusive language in the dressing room and on the bench. Two parents stated they were prepared to remove their sons from his team because of "problems with the coach."

2. A parent insisted his son should play as a forward despite the fact the young man's natural position, as decided by his coaches, was on defence. The player himself, a non-scorer, stated he preferred to play defence.

3. A parent insisted on blowing a whistle from the crowd whenever she felt her son's team needed an advantage, such as a stoppage of play. She continued to blow her whistle despite a plea from a coach to desist. The woman's husband assaulted the coach.

4. An unidentified female struck and injured a young referee with her purse, in which she had hidden a large rock.

5. A young woman, said to be the sister of a pee-wee player, spit at a referee as he left the dressing room after a game.

6. A coach was accused by league officials and other coaches of throwing pennies on the ice during games in an effort to create extra "rest time" for his first-string players. The same coach was accused of recruiting his family members to throw eggs on the ice to create "timeouts".

7. Two coaches of a peewee team, who supervised

the construction of an outdoor rink on the river, had all their efforts thwarted by a mean-spirited vandal or vandals who destroyed the rink by dumping sand and gravel on the surface. Local police say an investigation is underway, but no suspects have been identified.

8. An exhibition game between peewee teams played on an outdoor rink in Turtle Creek ended when a gang of rowdies attempted to beat up the two teenage coaches of the winning team. The coaches were saved from a mauling by the intervention of friends.

The list is sickening. It's a black mark on minor hockey in Indian River. And if it's happening here in the North Country, you can wager it's a problem that is national in scope. For heaven's sake, folks, let's come to our senses. This is kids' hockey, not the NHL. Most of the kids play for the joy and the thrill of the game. They learn about rules and regulations and, for the most part, willingly abide by them. They play because the game is fun! But it's not much fun to witness coaches throwing temper tantrums, or to hear them order players to "rip somebody's head off". Nor is it fun to see a player's mother hurl a weighted purse at a young referee's head, or spit on him, or call him "moron" and "imbecile".

Let's put a stop to these shenanigans! And let's do it now!

Everyone in Indian River read the *Review*, and most people respected the editor, Harry Mitchell. His editorial caused much comment and won widespread approval.

Of course, some oldtimers disagreed. One wrote a letter to the editor:

> *When we were young and played the game, it was brutal but we survived. And we loved it that way. We had guts. We ripped into each other and whaled away with our sticks and fists. It was a man's game then. And the referees were lucky to survive a season. A few wore hard hats during the games. Fans would throw bottles at them and puncture the tires on their cars. They left the rink after a game wearing their skates on their hands— to ward off any fans who might want to pummel them. In those days, we players were tough as nails. We had to be. Today's hockey is soft—tame by comparison.*

His letter brought a reply from a high-school teacher:

> *The correspondent who wrote about the brutality of old-time hockey should be dispatched to an old folks' home immediately where he can babble away to a deaf and dazed audience. We live in a civilized world now, and the time for players ripping into each other with sticks and fists and for*

*fans throwing bottles and other missiles at referees
is, hopefully, a shameful part of hockey's past.
Gone and good riddance! Today, such brutish
behaviour is repugnant to most thinking fans.
Wake up, parents! Take the game back from those
who spoil it by advocating violence and a "win at
all costs" attitude.*

Over the next few days, Harry Mitchell received
dozens of letters from readers of the *Review*. Most
heartily endorsed his call for a cleanup of minor
hockey in Indian River.

"If nothing else," he said at the breakfast table,
"it shows how connected most people are to
hockey. How passionate they are about the game.
I've never had such a response to one of my
editorials."

"There have been fewer incidents since you
wrote it," Max said. "None at our games."

"Well, there was one little thing," Marty added.
"Squirt was upset when his dad kept screaming at
him to hit someone on the other team. So he went
on a sit-down strike. It was a riot."

"He what?" asked their father.

"Yep," Marty said. "Squirt sat down on the ice
and said he wasn't moving until his dad quit
yelling at him. The referee stopped the play and
gave Squirt a minor penalty for delay of game. But
Squirt refused to go to the box. The fans thought

it was hilarious."

"What about Mr. Bragan, Squirt's dad? What did he do?"

"Oh, he was really embarrassed. He turned all red in the face. Fans started booing him. Then he ran out to the lobby—said he needed a coffee. Only after he left did Squirt decide to sit in the penalty box after all."

"Did his father come back?" their mother asked. "Or was he too ashamed?"

Marty chuckled. "Yep. He came back, but he stood in a far corner behind a post. Didn't say boo for the rest of the game. Mom, I think you're right. I think he was ashamed."

Harry Mitchell shook his head. "Boys, when I suggested earlier in the season that you'd make good coaches of a peewee team, I never dreamed you'd run into so many problems. It can't be much fun for you—or for the kids on your team."

"That's where you're wrong, Dad," Max said. "We're having tons of fun. Marty and I are coaching some of the best young kids around. They live and breathe hockey, just like we did at that age."

"And still do," Marty interjected.

"And most of the parents have been great, too," Max continued. "It feels so good when parents come up and thank us for helping their son play better hockey. And for teaching him some life skills, like showing respect for a referee and..."

"Or teaching her," Marty said. "Don't forget we've got a girl on the team. Mr. Falzone is so grateful that we signed his daughter, Nicole. He calls us groundbreakers and visionaries. He thinks that someday thousands of girls will be playing hockey. Maybe even in a pro league. What do you think, Dad?"

Their father laughed. "Don't ask me—ask your mother. She was a star player in her day."

"Mr. Falzone may be right," their mother said. "A pro league for women might be a stretch, but why not the Olympics? I'd love to be there when female players from different countries play at the Winter Olympics."

"Hey, when that happens, maybe Nicole will be in goal!" Marty suggested.

Max jumped in. "There's a headline for you, Dad: Nicole Falzone Brings Home Olympic Gold."

Marty rose to his feet and proclaimed, "Her coaches, Max and Marty Mitchell, share in Olympic glory."

Max leaped up beside his brother. "Thousands line parade route and throw confetti from skyscrapers as Indian River salutes Nicole Falzone."

"That's ridiculous," Harry Mitchell said between chuckles. "Skyscrapers in Indian River?"

Marty got in the last line: "Nicole attributes her gold-medal win to the genius of her coach—the renowned Marty Mitchell!"

Their father clapped his hands together. "That's enough fantasy for tonight," he said. "There's homework to be done. Now get to it, or one of my future stories might begin: Mitchell Brothers Flunk Out of School. Father and mother disown them and cut them out of their will. Boys say they'll begin careers as hobos and work their way up to being tramps."

CHAPTER 16

JUDGE GAUL TAKES CHARGE

There was a surprising announcement on the following day. Mr. Tremblay resigned as the league commissioner, citing failing health as the reason for the move. But his wife told a neighbour, "My husband was simply fed up with the problems he had to deal with daily in minor hockey."

Members of the hockey council met later that day in an effort to name a successor.

"Mr. Tremblay is irreplaceable," one member said gloomily. "There's simply not a soul in Indian River who can do the job." The others scratched their heads and nodded in agreement.

Harry Mitchell's voice barked through the gloom of silence that followed. "Oh, yes, there is—let's ask Judge Gaul if he'll take over."

It was a brilliant suggestion, although many felt the judge would decline the offer. He was far too busy to supervise a minor hockey league.

"Give the biggest jobs to the busiest men," Harry Mitchell said. "He can always say no."

But Judge Gaul said yes. "It'll be a pleasant diversion from my regular work," he said. "And I've always loved hockey. But mind you, what I say goes."

The judge quickly settled a few minor disputes and organized a playoff system for the teams in town. He convinced a local hardware store to donate money for trophies. Then he made some long-distance phone calls and accomplished a coup, something so totally unexpected that no one in town would have even considered it possible, much less attempted it. He arranged for the peewee champions of the town's four-team league to play in Quebec City—in a new tournament for the national championship.

Not all his pronouncements brought joy and approval. Reluctantly, he delivered a crushing blow to the River Rats, via a phone call to Max and Marty.

"I can't allow you to use Mr. Stanowski's farm pond as a practice rink any longer," he said. "I'm worried that the vandals who destroyed your rink on the river may be the same men who assaulted you the other day at Whizzer Wilson's place. They may be looking for more trouble and I'd prefer that you and your team be closer to town. I can arrange for some police patrols here. But I don't have much control over what happens elsewhere."

"Do you think it was Whizzer and his pals who ruined our rink in town?" Max asked the judge.

"Don't know. But I'd advise you to either return to your old rink, or build another one next to it. Let me know if I can help."

Max and Marty talked it over.

"The rink on the river was ideal," Max said. "Until someone dumped all that sand and gravel all over it. I don't know how we'd ever scrape it off."

Marty snapped his fingers. "What about the Cobras?" he asked. "They're our friends now."

"What about them? They're not going to want to shovel all that mess off the ice."

"Oh, yes, they are," Marty said excitedly. "And I'll tell you why."

Within 48 hours, the old rink on the river was free of sand and gravel, the ice had been restored to its original gleaming condition, the fish huts had been repaired after some vigorous hammering and nailing of fresh boards and the pot-bellied stoves were functional and spreading heat to all corners while plumes of white smoke curled lazily skyward out of their L-shaped chimneys.

"That's amazing," Tim Robbins said, as he led the River Rats back to their original home. "How in the world did you fellows accomplish it?"

"We've got the Cobras to thank," Max explained. "And my brother Marty. Marty remembered that the Cobras were planning to build a clubhouse in the spring. And they were going to build a cement floor. Good cement needs lots of sand and gravel, and what we had on our ice met their needs. So we gave it to them. They moved in yesterday and scraped it all up with a small bulldozer and a truck. And a lot of shovelling, of course. After that, the Cobras helped us lay several coats of water over the rink until— presto!—well, you can see. It's just like new."

"The players are thrilled," Tim said approvingly. "Now let's try it out."

"Hey, Tim," Marty called out, as the River Rats prepared to practice. "Maybe you'll win that trip to Quebec City after all."

A trip to Quebec was the kind of incentive that motivated all the peewee players in town—and the River Rats were no exception.

"I've always wanted to go to Quebec," Tim Robbins said. "I want to see the Plains of Abraham, where General Wolfe defeated General Montcalm. Miss Fallis gave me a book about the battle between the French and the English. Wolfe climbed a steep cliff with 5,000 men and took Montcalm and his troops by surprise. Both generals died within minutes of each other after the battle."

"To heck with all that history stuff," Chubby Morris snorted. "I want to go because they have a big indoor rink there. And I want to play on it."

Max told the River Rats not to set their hopes too high. A trip to Quebec was only possible if they won the league title. And that was unlikely. The first-place Steamrollers were the odds-on favourites to repeat as champions.

The River Rats failed to overtake the Steamrollers in the stretch run. But they finished a mere two points behind and had no trouble winning their initial playoff series in two straight games against the Wildcats. The Wildcats couldn't cope with the line of Tim Robbins and the Stanowski brothers, who accounted for all ten goals in the best-of-three series. The scores were 6–0 and 4–0. Nicole Falzone was a standout in goal, registering both shutouts.

Meanwhile, the Steamrollers flattened the fourth place Lumber Kings, also in two straight games, by scores of 10–1 and 8–2. After the series, Wally Wilson told a reporter, "I can't wait to crush the River Rats, my former team. They play sissy hockey. And they're badly coached. I've packed my suitcase and I'm practicing my French. 'Bonjour, mes amis. Je suis Wally.' How's that, Mr. Reporter?"

The best-of-three final series started off with the Steamrollers in full gear. A near-capacity crowd filled the 1,500-seat Indian River Arena for game one.

The bigger, stronger Steamrollers controlled the play in the first period and banged home the first goal. A harmless shot by Wally Wilson struck

Roddy Barnaby on the ankle and slowly deflected into the open corner of the net. It was the only goal of the period.

Wally Wilson couldn't resist taunting Nicole as the teams left the ice. "That was my popgun shot," he laughed. "Next period I'll show you my cannon shot. And in the third period, it'll be my howitzer."

"I'll be ready," Nicole promised. "All you've shown me so far is that you're good at shooting off at the mouth."

"Why you..." Wally snarled and lunged at Nicole. But Tim Robbins stepped between them and shouldered Wally out of the way. Wally staggered and almost fell. The referee, well aware of Wilson's history as a troublemaker, moved in and kept the players apart.

"Get to your dressing rooms," he thundered. "Or I'll toss you out of the game."

The second period was scoreless, and Max came away pleased with the efforts of the River Rats. "We played them even and Nicole was steady," he said in the dressing room. "If we score the next goal, hopefully early in the third period, we've got a chance to win."

The Stanowski twins knew the meaning of early. They led a dazzling rush in the opening minute of the period, and Lance potted the first River Rats goal at the 58-second mark, Larry and Tim assisting.

The wisdom of those energetic practices on the river ice began to pay dividends as the period wore on. The River Rats never seemed to tire, while the Steamrollers slowly lost some of their steam—and their enthusiasm. A large factor in the outcome was the River Rats' defensive play.

Every time a Steamroller swept in for a shot on goal, a River Rat popped up to knocked him off stride, to deflect a shot, to intercept a pass.

The hockey-wise fans nodded their approval at the disciplined play of the underdogs. They knew expert coaching when they saw it, and began to applaud the River Rats' determined and relentless play.

"The poor Steamrollers," grunted one oldtimer. "They could put the Pied Piper in their lineup and he'd be helpless against these pesky little Rats."

"They're fun to watch," his wife agreed. "Even though they're not spectacular."

The words were barely out of her mouth when something spectacular happened. And it happened to a most unspectacular little fellow. Tiny Squirt Bragan chased Wally Wilson in behind the River Rats' net, where he deftly poked the puck off Wilson's stick. The puck bounced up and landed squarely on the blade of Squirt's stick. "Golly," murmured Squirt, "that was lucky. Let's just see how far I can go with this."

And go he did! Whirling around the net, with the puck apparently glued to his stick blade, he dashed between three incoming forwards, who braked frantically and tried to turn back. He out-legged a weary Wilson, who trailed behind him. He looked up. Lo and behold, there was but one defenceman back.

That player, who obviously had never seen a forward toting a puck on his stick blade, made a wild swipe at Squirt, hoping to knock the puck loose. But Squirt ducked and, yes, squirted past the defender, leaving him dazed, bewildered and floundering on his feet. Like a whippet, Squirt flew at the goalie, Slippery Bill Sloan, and with a lacrosse-like shot, drilled the puck past him.

Bedlam!

The fans cheered their lungs out. They had never seen such a goal! And they cheered even louder when Squirt scored another, this time from the slot and in a more traditional manner. This one turned out to be the game-winner. When the buzzer sounded to end the match, Squirt was carried off on the shoulders of his teammates.

In the dressing room, Max shook Squirt by the hand and said, "You're amazing. I've never seen a player carry the puck on the blade of his stick the length of the rink. How did you do that?"

Squirt laughed and held up his stick. "It's all in the gum, Coach. I almost swallowed my gum out there when Wilson stepped into me. So I got rid of it. Stuck a big wad on the blade of my stick. And that's exactly where the puck landed. And stayed there somehow. That wouldn't happen again in a million years."

Squirt's famous goal earned him a couple of new nicknames, Spearmint and Gummy among them.

The opening game victory shattered the Steamrollers' confidence. They played much more tentatively in game two, and the River Rats outskated them and outscored them by a 5–0 margin.

It was a stunning victory for a team that couldn't win a game earlier in the season. Nicole collected another shutout and was declared the MVP of the series. Tim Robbins scored two of the goals, while Lance and Larry Stanowski collected one apiece. The fifth was scored by defensive standout Roddy Barnaby, his first of the season.

"I told you he was a goal scorer," Roddy's dad shrieked when the puck went in. "Maybe next season they'll play him on the wing where he belongs."

"Put a sock in it, Barnaby," a fan shouted at the excited parent. "Your son's a great defenceman. Accept it."

To Tim Robbins' surprise, Wally Wilson skated up to him after the game. "Nice game, Tim," he said. "You fellows deserved to win. How about trading sticks? You know, to keep as a souvenir. Mine was a gift from my uncle."

"Sure, Wally. That's a good idea. By the way,

you didn't play as rough in today's game. How come?"

"You're too polite, Tim. You mean I didn't play as dirty, don't you? I dunno—I never should have gone after Nicole, your goalie. She's a good kid and I was out of line. After the first game I got thinking about that editorial in the *Review*. It finally dawned on me that I'm one of the problems in hockey. But not anymore. At least I hope not."

"Glad to hear it, Wally," Tim said, extending his hand. "We're still friends?"

"You bet," Wally said. "And tell your coaches I miss them."

In the dressing room, after the victory celebration died down, Tim turned to Max.

"Wally Wilson gave me his stick after the game. But when I unrolled some tape from the shaft I saw your name on it. I can't figure it out."

Max examined the stick. "Why, it's the one I lost. Someone stole it out of the fish hut the night they ruined our rink. How did Wally get it?"

"His Uncle Whizzer gave it to him," Tim said. "His uncle must have been the one who stole it. You want it back you can have it."

"No, you keep it, Tim. But thanks. Now I'm certain I know who dropped all that sand and gravel all over our ice."

CHAPTER 17

OFF TO QUEBEC

The old wooden platform in front of the station creaked and sagged under the weight of at least 100 people. Less than half that number clutched tickets for the journey to Quebec City, for the return rail fare alone cost ten dollars. The rest were friends and relatives of the players, there to bid the River Rats "au revoir" and "bonne chance"—goodbye and good luck.

The River Rats had worked hard collecting money for the trip by selling chocolate bars door to door and holding a raffle with a new bicycle as a prize.

The players, proudly wearing bright red team jackets and matching red peaked caps donated by the Gray Paper Mill, held tightly to suitcases. Some clutched brown paper bags filled with sandwiches and cookies. The River Rats stood out in the middle of the crowd. Every few seconds, one would stand on tiptoes, staring down the track looking for the train.

Then someone shouted, "Here she comes!" and within minutes the train, as long as a city block and pulled by a huge locomotive, shuddered and wheezed to a stop at the station.

There was a mad rush to climb on board, to scramble for seats by the windows, to throw luggage in the bins overhead, to wave farewell to friends who remained behind.

When all were settled, Squirt Bragan shouted out, "Let's go! Let's get 'la grande aventure' underway." Squirt had been practicing his French phrases, and he wanted to show off in front of his teammates.

One might easily have assumed that the engineer in his striped coveralls, railroad cap and oil-stained gloves heard Squirt's call for action. Levers were pulled, there was a hiss of steam and a mighty blast of the horn signalled imminent departure. Conductors hustled to slam the doors separating the cars. The engineer looked back and tipped his cap to the crowd as his train glided away from the station.

"Au revoir, mes amis!" Squirt shouted, as he waved through the murky glass of a window.

"Hey, Squirt," Roddy Barnaby called out as the train moved faster. "Where'd you learn to speak French?"

"Marty's been teaching me. He's started taking French in school. When I get to Quebec I'm going to say, 'Que vous êtes belle,' to everyone I meet. It means, "Gosh, are you pretty."

"Better just say it to the girls," Roddy cautioned.

"And if we go to a French restaurant, Marty told me to say, 'Donnez-moi l'addition, s'il vous plaît.' It means, 'Give me your special, please.'"

Roddy roared with laughter. "It does not. It means, 'Give me the bill, please.' Marty's not the only one taking French at school."

All the River Rats laughed at Squirt, who looked puzzled.

"How about, 'Tu es complètement débile'?" he asked Roddy. "Marty says it means, 'You're a good player.' He told me to say it to all the players on the other teams."

Roddy laughed even harder. He slapped his knee and made the translation. "You goofball, Squirt. It means, 'You're a complete moron.'"

"Why, that Marty...!" Squirt began. Then he leaped from his seat and made his way down the aisle to where Marty was sitting next to Max. Marty saw him coming and quickly pulled his cap down over his eyes, pretending to be asleep. Squirt punched him on the shoulder and shouted in his ear. "Hey, Marty. Here's what I think of you. Tu es complètement débile!"

Then he turned and ran.

Max turned to Marty, who was grinning, pleased with himself for the practical joke he'd pulled on Squirt.

"You're always playing jokes on people, Marty. One day it'll backfire on you. It all started that time when Aunt Gertrude came to visit. You were just a kid."

Marty chuckled and said, "You're right. Mom might have sent me to my room that day—if she hadn't been laughing so hard."

Now Max began to chuckle, thinking of the incident.

"You told Aunt Gertrude that you wanted to play doctor but you were sad because you had no patients to examine. Remember?"

"Sure do. How could I forget?"

Max said, "Aunt Gertrude said she'd be your patient. So you filled small bottles with chunks of breakfast cereal and you made potions out of coloured water."

Marty laughed. "Yeah. And then I was ready to treat Aunt Gertrude. The whole family was there that day. She pretended to be ill. She said, 'Oh, doctor, I'm so sick.' Remember how she took my hand and placed it on her brow. 'Help me, doctor,' she groaned."

Max began to laugh out loud. "I'll never forget it," he chortled as tears formed in his eyes.

"The first thing I did was ask her to stick out her tongue. What a long tongue she had. When she stuck it out, I grabbed it and pulled on it—really hard.

"'Nothing wrong with your tongue, Aunt Gertrude,' I told her."

"Then you told her you had to clean her tongue off," Max said. "So you squirted lemon juice all over it. She almost jumped out of her chair."

"I thought of using soap and water," Marty snorted, "but the lemon juice worked. Her reaction was hilarious."

"And then you took her pulse," Max reminded his brother.

"That's right. I held her wrist and timed her pulse on my watch. When I told her it was beating 200 times a minute, she almost jumped out of the chair again. And that's when—poof—she farted."

"Poor Aunt Gertrude. She was so embarrassed. You remember what happened after that?"

"Course I do. Aunt Gertrude asked me what I thought was wrong with her. I said, 'Oh, Aunt Gertrude, you need a laxative. You haven't had a bowel movement in weeks.'"

"And that's when everybody started laughing—even Aunt Gertrude."

Marty opened a paper bag. "You want a cookie, Max? One of my fans baked them for me."

"Sure." Max bit down and almost cracked a tooth. The cookie didn't crumble—it was hard as a brick. He tossed the cookie back in the bag.

"Hang onto them, Marty," he chuckled. "We may

need them if we ever run short of pucks."

Marty suddenly sat up straight and craned his head, looking down the aisle.

"There's Mr. Stanowski sitting a few seats ahead of us. He's sitting with the twins, with his back to us. But who's the blond lady sitting next to him?"

"Don't know. But Miss Fallis is going to be upset if he's got a new lady in his life."

"Let's go see," Marty said.

Max and Marty were striding nonchalantly down the aisle when the blond lady turned her head slightly, showing her profile.

"Wow! She's good looking," Max whispered. "Mr. Stanowski's a lucky guy. I wonder who she is."

"Poor Miss Fallis," Marty murmured. "I know she was hoping..."

They were pushing forward when the woman rose from her seat and turned toward them, almost bumping into them.

"Hello, Max. Hello, Marty. I didn't see you two when we boarded the train. I'm so excited about going to Quebec."

Max and Marty were stunned.

"Miss Fallis! Is it really you?" Max stammered.

"We didn't recognize you," Marty added. "You've changed. You're...you're...beautiful."

Miss Fallis laughed and tossed her head.

"Thank you," she said. "I had my hair done. No more buns in the back, and I had it coloured. And

I bought some makeup. New glasses, too. Silas seems to like the new me."

"We do too," Marty said.

"I liked you just as much before you coloured your hair, Stella," Silas called out.

"I was just about to take off my gloves," Miss Fallis said. "Wait'll you see."

She pulled a glove off her left hand and held up her fingers.

"My gosh!" Max exclaimed. "A diamond ring. Does that mean...?"

Miss Fallis giggled like a schoolgirl.

"It does," she said. "Silas and I are engaged. We're going to be married."

"That's great news," Marty said, reaching to shake her hand. "Congratulations, Miss Fallis. Now the twins will have a new mother."

"Joe, too," she reminded them. "But I'm not replacing their mother, Marty. I'll be their step-mother. And they seem pretty happy about it."

Hoot! Hooooot!

The howl of the train whistle drowned out further talk. It was as if the engineer had overheard their conversation and was sending his congratulations to the happy librarian.

CHAPTER 18

FRENCH CULTURE

Hours later, after much banter and giggling and, of course, a trip to the dining car, the players realized they were getting closer to their destination. They had stopped for an hour in Montreal and were allowed to leave the train to stretch their legs and look around.

They were amazed at the hustle and bustle they witnessed on the streets of the huge city. They craned their necks to look at all the tall buildings.

"Montreal is almost 300 years old," Max told the players. "It's the second-largest French-speaking city in the world."

"I wish we could visit the Montreal Forum," someone said. "My favourite NHL team plays there—the Canadiens."

But there was no time for a trip to the Forum. The train rolled on, and soon the conductor strolled through the cars, alerting passengers to the stops ahead by ringing a small bell.

"Repentigny next. Then Sorel. Then Cap-de-la-

Madeleine and Sainte Foy. And our final stop—Quebec City."

"I'm glad we don't live in one of those places," Squirt quipped. "It would take me a year to learn how to pronounce the name of my home town."

"Keep working on your French, Squirt," Marty advised him. "And when we get to Quebec City, be sure to greet everybody by saying, 'Tu es grossi.'"

"Oh, no. You're not going to fool me again, Marty," answered Squirt. "I bought a French phrase book at the station in Montreal." He flipped through the pages. "And I'm glad I did. 'Tu es grossi' means 'You've put on weight.' No more French lessons from you, Marty. You can't be trusted."

When the train shuddered to a halt at the station in Quebec City, players, family and friends disembarked and were greeted by one Romeo Lebel, organizer of the tournament.

"Bienvenue! Bienvenue!" he shouted in greeting. "Thank you for coming. Is it true you are called River Rats? A strange name for a team, but..." He shrugged and continued, "Some of our French names must sound strange to you as well. Come with me. We have horse-drawn sleighs waiting to take you to your hotel. Then we will embark on a tour of the city. Tomorrow you play in the first game of the tournament. You will meet a team from Gaspé."

After checking in at a small hotel near the arena, the River Rats jumped back on the sleighs and were escorted around the famous city. Romeo Lebel, acting as tour guide, proudly pointed out the scenic wonders of his city.

"You will find no place like this in all of North America," he proclaimed. "Old Quebec is set on terraces of land next to the mighty St. Lawrence River. It is the only walled city in North America and it is four centuries old, discovered by Jacques Cartier in 1535. Almost all of the 500 thousand natives of Quebec City speak French. But many can speak some English, too, if they are smart like me," he said, grinning broadly and tapping his big chest.

"But didn't the English take the city from the French in a big battle?" Squirt called out. "Miss Fallis loaned me a book about Quebec."

"Oui, I'm sorry to say they did," Mr. Lebel replied. "But it was not a big battle. It lasted only half an hour. That was in 1759, when that rascal, General Wolfe, sneaked up the cliffs with his troops and surprised us—I mean he surprised General Montcalm, the French commander. Generals—like goaltenders—must not be caught sleeping. Both men died of wounds suffered in the battle."

Romeo Lebel waved a finger at his captive audience. "General Wolfe took our city but he could never erase our language. We have continued speaking it ever since the guns stopped firing."

"Why is the city called Quebec?" Marty asked.

"Mon ami," said Mr. Lebel, "the name 'Quebec' comes from 'Kebec' in the Algonquin language. So it was originally an Indian name and it means 'Where the river narrows.'"

"During our tour," he continued, "you will see many churches, monuments and historical sites. We will stroll through cobblestoned streets—one of them the oldest street in North America. We'll visit the oldest commercial district and see the oldest church on the continent. You will hear the ringing of church bells and savour the smells of French cuisine."

"That means French cooking," Squirt said knowingly. "Cuisine means a style of cooking. I looked it up."

"C'est correct," nodded Mr. Lebel. "And we will tour La Citadelle, a star-shaped fortress located above the city. Finally, we'll pass a most memorable landmark, the copper-green and turreted Château Frontenac Hotel. Can you guess why you're not staying there?"

"Costs too much," a chorus of voices responded.

"Absolument," nodded Romeo Lebel. "Well, maybe next time..."

"Now we will take you for a fine meal of tourtière, patates frites or—if you prefer—our famous crêpes. Then it'll be time for bed. Big game tomorrow against the Gaspé Galleons."

CHAPTER 19

WHIZZER SHOWS UP

"There are only four teams in the tournament," Max said to Marty after the River Rats left their cramped, stuffy dressing room and trooped out on the ice of the rundown arena that held less than 2,000 fans. They were about to meet a fleet team of peewees from the Gaspé region.

"How come only four teams?" Marty asked. "I thought there would be more. This is hardly a national tournament."

"Two teams from the West cancelled out," Max explained. "They couldn't raise enough money to travel east. It's too bad—they have some great teams out west. It would have been fun to play against them.

"The other three clubs here are going to be tough to beat. There's the Gaspé club, the Quebec City team and a team from Halifax. We're the only representative from the North Country. Tonight, Quebec meets Halifax in the second game.

"These tournaments for kids are something new

in hockey, but Mr. Lebel says they are going to be wildly popular someday—especially here in Quebec City. He says someday they'll draw dozens of teams and thousands of fans."

"That's hard to believe," Marty scoffed. "Thousands of people watching peewees play? Come on. There's only a couple of hundred fans in the rink today."

"That makes us pioneers, I guess," Max responded, heading for the door. "Well, let's go out and see if the River Rats can have a little beginner's luck."

But it would take more than luck to get past the Gaspé Galleons. From the drop of the puck, it was obvious the Galleons possessed speed in abundance and plenty of grit. And the crowd, as expected, cheered them on in French and English.

"Nicole looks a little shaky," Max observed after two rushes wound up in her crease and she juggled a bouncing puck in her glove.

"Small wonder," Marty replied, calling for a line change after the first minute of play. "She's a pioneer, too. No girl has ever played in any peewee tournament, as far as I know."

The momentum changed when the Stanowski twins and Tim Robbins took their first shift. Some clever passing by the trio moved the puck into the Galleons' zone. Tim's low, hard shot on net was scooped up by Gingras, the opposing goaltender.

"Good shift, boys! Good shift!" shouted Miss Fallis, clapping her hands. Parents and fans who'd come on the trip followed her lead and applauded wildly.

Several minutes of fast-paced, exciting hockey followed, with the peewees skimming over the ice like painted water bugs, chasing the puck, chasing each other, chasing after goals—but without success.

The goaltending was sensational. Nicole settled down and crouched over her pads, determined to act most unladylike if she had to, determined to prove she belonged on the same ice with the bigger, tougher boys. At the other end, Gingras, a tall lad with long arms, swallowed pucks with his gloved hand.

"He's like a bullfrog gulping down bugs," Marty observed.

"Don't call him a frog," Max cautioned. "Not in Quebec."

"I didn't mean anything by it," Marty said defensively.

Tim Robbins also commented on Gingras' skill. "It's like shooting pucks into a bushel basket," he complained, after three of his shots disappeared into that big glove.

The first period ended scoreless.

So did the second period.

But in the third, tiny Nicole Falzone upstaged

her goaltending rival, who relied perhaps too much on his magic glove.

She used stick, pads and glove to ward off Galleon attacks. The Gaspé speedsters flashed in time after time, only to be frustrated by the little lady in the baseball catcher's mask. She stopped a dozen shots and then, perhaps in desperation, she fired a rebound with her stick up the ice to Lance Stanowski. He snapped up the long pass, wheeled and relayed the puck to his brother Larry. Larry whipped the disc ahead to a streaking Tim Robbins. In full stride, Tim would not and could not be caught. He raced in on Gingras and drilled a scoring shot to the high corner—stick side.

"I was tired of sinking shots into his big glove," Tim said later, after the goal stood up and the River Rats had won the game. "It was great to score the game-winner. And Nicole played a big role in the goal—even though she wasn't given an assist."

"Nicole saved the game for us at one end and Tim won it for us at the other," Max told the lone reporter who was covering the tournament for a Quebec newspaper. "We're happy to get off to a good start. Tonight we'll watch Quebec play Halifax."

One can only imagine how stunned Max and Marty were when they returned to the arena hours later. They could not have been more shocked if someone had thrown a toaster or a radio into their bath water—while they were sitting in it.

There on the ice were the Quebec City boys, warming up at one end of the rink. They looked to be a poised team of youngsters wearing flashy blue-and-white uniforms. But at the other end...

"That's not the Halifax team!" Max said incredulously. "Why, those boys are from..."

"Turtle Creek!" howled Marty. "But how? Why? What are the Terrors doing here?"

Romeo Lebel hurried over to explain. "There was a last minute change." He shrugged and sighed. "Halifax cancelled out. Seven of their players came down with the flu. A man named Wilson called me. Somehow he heard about the cancellation. He said he had a good peewee team headed for an exhibition game in Montreal, and he'd postpone the game there if I'd let him replace Halifax. Said his team was every bit as good as the River Rats. What could I do? I was desperate to have a fourth entry. I said, 'Hurry, Mr. Wilson. Come to Quebec. Bless you, my good fellow.'"

"Hmmm. You're blessing him now, but you may wind up cursing him," Marty muttered under his breath. "He's a big troublemaker."

"What's that, Marty?" Mr. Lebel asked. "I didn't hear."

"Oh, nothing," Marty said, smiling brightly at Mr. Lebel. "You've got your fourth team, Mr. Lebel.

I'm sure they'll bring a lot of, well, excitement to the tournament."

In the game that followed, the unknown team from Turtle Creek displayed a brand of hockey that was entirely familiar to the River Rats, but totally unfamiliar to the fans in Quebec. It was rough. It was crude. And it was effective. Turtle Creek's aggressive play left the Quebec boys battered and in tatters.

The taller, stronger and possibly older farm boys, with their boorish coach waving his cigar like a baton and urging his hellions to "hammer those little Frenchmen" skated to a 10–0 victory. It was three periods of torture for the Quebecers, who were slashed and belted at every turn. They were pummelled when they were down and punished unmercifully when they were upright. The increasing number of boos and catcalls from the crowd seemed to further inflame the visitors, whose coach ran back and forth hurling insults and abusive language at players, fans and officials.

His nephew Wally, whom he'd recruited for the trip, was the only visiting player to look on in dismay.

When several irate fathers of the Quebec players moved menacingly in his direction, Whizzer turned them back with wild swings of a hockey stick. And he laughed at them. Eventually, four burly policemen protected him from bodily harm. After the game, he sneered, "I'm as tough behind the bench as I am as a player. Was I frightened of those parents? Not for a second. They were pussycats. I would have flattened 'em all by myself."

Mr. Lebel was stunned.

"Never did I expect such boorish behaviour," he wailed after the humiliating defeat to the home-town team. "Never, never, never! It was so...so ugly! And uncalled for. The Quebec coach is so upset he says he'll concede his next game rather than play another team from the North Country. That means he'll concede to you fellows. He is devastated and most of his players are badly beaten up. That ignorant man Wilson is a disgrace to hockey—and to your part of the country. To think that an hour ago I was blessing him for coming to the help of my tournament." Mr. Lebel turned away, a tear forming in one eye.

"We could have told you about Whizzer Wilson, Mr. Lebel," Max said sympathetically. "We've seen his act before. It's shameful. I wish you'd taken time to ask us about him."

"But I was desperate. I never dreamed..."

"He's a disgrace in the North Country, too," added Marty. He sighed. "Now what are you going to do, Mr. Lebel?"

"I must talk to Mr. Wilson. His team will play Gaspé tomorrow afternoon. I must plead with him to show more sportsmanship for the rest of the tournament and to consider the importance of building good relations between French Canada and English Canada."

"And if Turtle Creek wins tomorrow, they'll meet us in the championship game on Saturday. Is that the deal, Mr. Lebel?"

"Oui. That is what will happen, now that Quebec has pulled out. Unless you plan to desert us, too. But please don't do that. Then I am ruined. This tournament is only the beginning. In years to come there will be much bigger, better tournaments. With many, many teams. If you pull out..."

"We won't desert you, Mr. Lebel," Max reassured him. "We're not all like Whizzer Wilson in the North Country. Besides, we believe in what you're doing. We want you to succeed."

"Not that we're anxious to play Turtle Creek on Saturday," Marty said. "Not with a maniac behind their bench. Besides, we have to worry about the well-being of our players. Our boys have a lot of courage but Turtle Creek plays vicious hockey, really dirty hockey, as you've seen. And there's only one man to blame for it."

"Whizzer Wilson," Romeo Lebel groaned aloud. "I wish I had never heard that man's name."

CHAPTER 20
A DISGRACEFUL PERFORMANCE

On Friday morning, a large photo of Whizzer Wilson wielding a hockey stick and swinging it viciously at a number of parents caused a sensation in Quebec City's major newspaper.

"Look at that!" Marty said to Max over breakfast. "Another black mark for kids' hockey." He read the article that accompanied the photo. "The reporter calls for Whizzer to be suspended."

"Good. What does our friend Romeo say to that?" Max asked.

"Says here Mr. Lebel met with Quebec hockey officials last night. They talked about a suspension. But Whizzer hired a lawyer who insisted his client was acting in self-defence. And if Whizzer is suspended, he threatens to sue the minor hockey association for a million dollars. The minor hockey people are going to meet again on the weekend to discuss the matter."

"Sure, they'll decide what to do when the tournament is over," Max shrugged. "Too late.

Whizzer's not going to care if they suspend him then. He'll be back home in Turtle Creek."

"Wonder if Romeo's plea to Whizzer to show more sportsmanship against Gaspé in today's game did any good," Marty said, looking up.

"I doubt it," Max replied. "But let's go out to the rink and see for ourselves."

The boys from the Gaspé had never played a roughhouse club like Turtle Creek before, and it showed in their tentative approach. In the opening period, they kept their heads up and skated gingerly, alert for any ugliness. It would be unfair to call them afraid, but they did appear to be somewhat nervous.

Behind the Turtle Creek bench, Whizzer Wilson pranced and smiled, enjoying the notoriety that followed the crude, intimidating hockey strategy he preached, the style that brought his team victory against Quebec City on the previous afternoon.

"Don't hit the little sissies," he bellowed for all to hear. "They'll run home to their mammies."

The crowd, much bigger on this day because of the negative publicity Whizzer had received overnight, booed him lustily.

They howled in patriotic outrage later in the period when he pulled a Quebec flag adorned with a fleur-de-lys from his pocket and pretended he was going to set it afire with his cigar.

"Oh my, they're angry," Max noted. "He's such a buffoon."

"The crowd will set him on fire if he's not careful," said Max. "Now the police are moving in to keep the fans away."

Wilson's antics took most of the focus away from the game, which plodded along at a snail's pace for 40 minutes. No score. The fans longed for a Gaspé goal. One goal would be like a gag pushed deep into the throat of the obnoxious coach behind the visitors' bench.

At the end of the second period, Wilson held up two fingers and made a circle with the fingers in his other hand.

"He's telling them his team will win by a 2–0 score," Max said. "He's taunting them. What arrogance!"

"What a jerk," echoed Marty.

"I feel sick about our fellows meeting Turtle Creek in tomorrow's game," Max said. "I sure hope Gaspé can pull it out today."

Early in the third period, Gaspé made a determined bid to win. They barged into the Turtle Creek zone and made some energetic efforts to score.

"Gutsy," said Max approvingly.

But Coach Wilson ordered his players to form a blockade in front of his goalie. "Hurt them, boys! Play 'em ugly!" he shrieked.

And the visiting Terrors turned into animals.

They mauled the smaller Gaspé players, hooked at them, tripped them, hauled them down and then fell on top heavily, crushing them with superior weight, using sticks to menace, do damage, create fear.

"I can't watch," Marty groaned, hiding his face in his hands.

There were whistles and penalties. And more boos. The infractions were obvious, but Whizzer Wilson just laughed at the parade to the penalty box. He recognized signs of defeat in an opponent when he saw it. He knew the Gaspé boys were discouraged and deflated. Out of gas.

"Now sic 'em," shrieked Wilson and his Terrors struck for two quick goals.

"That's enough," he barked, carelessly throwing his cigar butt over a shoulder into the crowd where it struck a young boy on the arm, leaving a burn mark. "We'll save some goals for those little rats in tomorrow's final."

The game ended and the crowd jumped up and directed a final loud razzing at the mouthy coach from the North Country.

Wilson patted each of his players on the back as they left the ice. They dodged and weaved their way through a barrage of debris—programs, candy wrappers, hats and coins. Wilson bent down to pick up some coins. And some jelly beans, which he popped into his mouth.

Chuckling and smiling, goading the fans, he stood on the bench and called for more. "Got a dollar and 75 cents so far," he hollered. Then he raised his arms—two fingers raised from one fist, a circle formed by fingers in the other.

"That was the score, folks," he roared. "Just as I predicted. Piece of cake, if you dolts know what that means."

He ducked a flying shoe rubber, snagged a quarter that flew in his direction with one hand and ran after his players to the dressing room.

CHAPTER 21

LAST CHANCE FOR THE RIVER RATS

"This is the end of our season, boys," Max said quietly to the players, who listened intently. With his hands deep in his pockets, Max paced the floor of the dressing room. "Marty and I are really sorry it has to end with a game against Turtle Creek. You know what's going to happen out there in the next hour, don't you? There's not much we can do about it. But we don't want you getting hurt. Look out for all the dirty tricks they'll be throwing at you."

"And take care of your goaltender," Marty advised, interrupting. "Protect Nicole at all costs. We understand if you're concerned about what might happen. And you should be concerned. These guys are bigger than you, maybe even tougher than you. And they play dirty because their coach orders them to. But I'll tell you this. They are not any better than you."

"They may even be older than you," Max said, "and be using doctored birth certificates. We don't know that for sure. But Marty's right. They are not better than you and never will be. You fellows have something they don't have. You have class. And you play with class. Marty and I are so proud to be your coaches. We've seen you come from a team with no wins and not much hope to a team that's one of the best in the nation in your age group. That's amazing. You should give yourselves a big cheer."

The River Rats promptly cheered for themselves.

"How about a cheer for Max and Marty?" Tim Robbins said. "They're the best coaches in the world."

The cheers echoed off the walls of the cramped dressing room.

"Now go out there and represent the North Country with pride," Max ordered, clapping his hands together.

"Give it your best," Marty added. "To us, you are the best."

To the surprise of the Mitchell brothers and their players, when they emerged from the corridor leading to the team benches, they saw that every seat in the arena was filled. Small kids hung precariously from the steel girders, and standing room was at a premium.

"I'll tell you, Whizzer Wilson knows how to attract an audience," Max muttered. "Imagine! A mostly French-speaking crowd coming out to see two English teams."

Then the puck was dropped and the game was underway. The pace was much quicker than witnessed in the previous day's game.

"I'm glad we started Robbins and the Stanowski twins," Max said to Marty over the roar of the crowd. "We'll find out soon enough if the Terrors can keep up with them."

The Terrors couldn't keep up, but they knew how to keep the River Rats down. The rough play began immediately. Hard bodychecks and hooks and slashes threw the River Rats off balance, disrupting their rhythm.

But when the Terrors stole the puck away and started a rush, the River Rats backchecked furiously. The Turtle Creekers ganged in front of the goal, jostling and elbowing for position, their sticks flying perilously close to Nicole. Chubby Thomas and Roddy Barnaby, both of whom had improved immensely over the season, stepped in with gusto and flattened a pair of intruding forwards.

"Thanks, guys," Nicole said through her baseball mask. "Isn't this fun?"

Craig Carnegie, the toughest of the Terrors, decided to test the mettle of the high-stepping River Rats' first line with a sneak attack before the period ended. He blocked a pass, and then waited for Tim Robbins to attempt to steal the puck from between his feet. When Tim reached for the puck, Carnegie slashed his stick across Tim's forearm. Tim howled in pain and slumped to the ice, his head in his arms.

"Two minutes. Slashing!" barked the referee.

Carnegie laughed. He leaned over Tim and said, "Yer fakin'."

Chubby Thomas raced across the ice and was about to barrel into Carnegie when he remembered his coach's advice. "No retaliation penalties!" He veered away at the last instant. *Stay cool,* he told himself.

"Way to go, Carnegie!" Whizzer Wilson called from the bench. "Two minutes is worth it if it takes Robbins out of the game."

After a few minutes, with the help of his team-mates, Tim struggled to his feet and made his way to the River Rats' dressing room. The public-address announcer called for a doctor to come to the room immediately.

Meanwhile, the penalty timekeeper did a double take when Carnegie threw himself down on the bench next to him. "This kid looks like he's ready to shave," he muttered to himself. "He's the oldest-looking 12-year-old I've ever seen."

The goalies performed brilliantly. Tim Robbins failed to return to the ice after the hit from Carnegie. The period ended in a scoreless tie.

In the second period, Carnegie tried to goad little Squirt into a fight. "I'll mop up the ice with you, you midget," Carnegie threatened, throwing off a glove and thrusting a big fist in Squirt's face.

Squirt grabbed the fist with one hand and held on. Then he shook it up and down. "And how are you tonight, Mr. Carnegie," said Squirt, smiling innocently. "Why, you look older than my father. But your breath is much worse. Yuck!" Then he surprised Carnegie by taking his big thumb and twisting it. Carnegie howled in pain and jumped back. Impulsively, he stuck his sore thumb in his mouth.

Squirt acted surprised. "I did that too when I was a baby," he said. "But only until I stopped wearing diapers. Are you still wearing diapers, Carnegie?"

Fans along the rail laughed loudly at the exchange.

Carnegie made a wild lunge at Squirt, but Squirt ducked in behind the referee.

"Here I am," Squirt called out, peering around the referee's elbow. "Catch me if you can." He darted away with Carnegie in furious pursuit. Squirt fled across the ice. He dashed through the gate to the team bench just as Carnegie closed in. Squirt slammed the gate shut and Carnegie, skating at top speed, slammed into the barrier.

Wham!

Carnegie hit the gate with his mid-section and the collision knocked all the breath out of him. He staggered and would have fallen had not the River Rats reached out from the bench to offer helping hands. They held him upright while they massaged his head and face with their gloves. They pulled his hair and tugged on his ears until the referee came to Carnegie's aid. When he arrived, Squirt was extracting two fingers from Carnegie's nostrils and Carnegie was squealing in pain.

"I can't give the River Rats a penalty for ear-pulling," the referee told his linesman. "Or for hair-ruffling."

"And certainly not for nostril-filling," the linesman replied with a grin. "Besides, it was the big lunkhead's fault he got into this mess."

"Play hockey!" the referee barked. Then he turned and locked eyes with Squirt. He winked and said, "No more nonsense from you."

Squirt smiled and nodded. "Yes, sir."

The game continued, with some excellent play-making and a dozen scoring chances at each end of the rink. Several attempts by the Terrors to batter the Stanowski twins into the ice failed miserably. Why? Because the twins were as slippery as seals and could not be caught.

When the period ended, neither team had scored.

During the second intermission, the emotions

in the respective dressing rooms made a stark contrast.

Max and Marty praised their players.

"Doin' well, boys. And Nicole. Doin' real well," Marty shouted with enthusiasm. "This will be the period they'll come after you. They'll try to get you mad."

"Stay cool," urged Max. "Don't retaliate. Remember, you've got more character than they have."

In the other room, Whizzer Wilson tore into his players. "Yer not playing tough enough. You've got to knock the bejabbers out of 'em. He followed up with some language that even his veteran players hadn't heard before. And he finished by saying, "I want this championship, boys. I want to be able to go home and show the folks in Indian River what a real coach looks like—a winning coach. Now get out there and win it for me!"

Carnegie whispered to Wally Wilson as they left the room, "Your uncle is getting a little carried away, isn't he? He's made it pretty clear he wants this win for himself—not for us."

"I'm disgusted," Wally replied. "I used to believe in his methods, but not anymore. It's no fun playing for him, and after tonight I won't play for him again."

CHAPTER 22

THE FINAL PERIOD

Twenty minutes to play! A scoreless game with the tournament title on the line.

"This is it, Marty," Max said. "The end of our season. Wilson will throw everything but the kitchen sink at our boys, and we're missing a key player. The doc is still examining Tim Robbins' arm."

"Don't worry about it," Marty responded. "The River Rats can win with or without Tim. Turtle Creek's got the clout but we've got the character."

Max had an inspiration. "I want to move Chubby Thomas up to the forward line. He can replace Tim. He's tough and fearless and the Turtle Creek kids will think twice about going after the Stanowski twins with Chubby there to look out for them."

"Good idea," said Marty.

It was a revelation for Chubby to play with the slick-passing Stanowskis. In the first five minutes of play, he had two superb scoring chances and was so surprised when the short passes clicked on the blade of his stick that he muffed both of his shots, shooting wide.

"That won't happen again," he vowed. "Just give me another chance, fellows."

Meanwhile, Chubby had business to attend to in the corner. A Turtle Creek player walloped Larry Stanowski into the boards with a clean but hard check. Larry dropped to the ice like a sack of potatoes. Chubby raced over and went face to face with the checker.

"Do that again and I'll knock you into...into the Plains of Abraham," Chubby threatened.

"The what?" asked the confused defender.

"The Plains of Abraham, you dummy," Chubby repeated. "I'll beat you like Wolfe whipped Montcalm."

"Never heard of those guys," muttered the Turtle Creek player, skating away.

When play resumed, Chubby made good on his promise to the twins. Lance and Larry raced into the Turtle Creek zone, displayed some fancy passing and finished off a play in front of the net with a quick pass to Chubby. He made no mistake this time, and popped the puck into the upper corner of the net.

"Yippee!" he shrieked. "My first goal! And it could be a game-winner!" He danced around the ice and embraced the Stanowskis.

The crowd went wild. There was no mistaking which team they favoured.

When Chubby skated to the River Rats' bench, his teammates mobbed him. Among the smiling faces was Tim Robbins.

"I'll take over, champ," Tim said. "Doc found nothing but a big bruise on my arm. Besides, we need you back on defence."

"Then I'd better get the puck I scored with," Chubby said, turning to retrieve it from the referee. "That may have been the only goal I'll ever score."

"Come on! Come on! Play hockey!" screamed Whizzer Wilson. "Stop stallin'!"

The bilingual linesman skated close to the Turtle Creek bench and told Wilson in French to put a sock in it.

"Huh?" cried Wilson. "What's that supposed to mean?"

If the goal by Chubby Thomas didn't take the starch out of the Terrors, a second one by Tim Robbins surely did.

And the roughhouse tactics of the Turtle Creekers vanished completely after Wally Wilson was hit by a stick and knocked unconscious.

Strangely, his own coach wielded the stick.

This hockey rarity took place after Tim Robbins' goal. Whizzer Wilson screamed that Robbins was offside. He flew into a tantrum when the referee declared the goal perfectly legal. Wilson threw water bottles on the ice and then raised a stick and hurled it at the referee like a javelin. But his nephew Wally, who raced over in a vain attempt to prevent his uncle from causing further damage, was struck across the face by the missile. He collapsed, bleeding from a cut over his eye.

A hush fell over the crowd. Young Wilson did not move for several seconds. It took his coach almost that long to realize what a horrible thing he had done, to acknowledge what a fool he had been.

He rushed to his nephew's side, sick with remorse. But a doctor shouldered him out of the way. "Go away!" the doctor commanded. "You've done enough damage. I'm in charge here."

When Wilson moved slowly back to the team bench, he was reviled by the crowd, subjected to the loudest chorus of boos he'd ever heard.

Fans hurled insults, toe rubbers and programs at him. The ice around him was soon cluttered with debris.

Max and Marty, seething like the rest, witnessed Wilson suddenly stand and do something that astonished them both. He pleaded with the crowd for forgiveness. Over the jeers that rained down, he cried out, "I'm sorry. I'm so sorry. I'm the worst coach ever. The worst. And I'll never coach again."

"Did you hear that?" Max asked, poking his brother on the arm. "He's actually apologizing."

Nobody else heard Wilson's plea. Nobody cared. Head down, he shuffled away, the catcalls ringing in his ears.

He passed the dressing room door and peeked in. The doctor was busy applying stitches to Wally's face.

"You okay, Wally?" he asked his nephew.

Wally was stretched out on a table. He glanced over, blinking. "I'm okay. I'll see you later."

The coach walked through the lobby. Two fans recognized him and jumped out of his way, treating him like an ogre. Behind his back, they snarled insults at him in French.

The roar of the crowd told him the game had continued. It would soon be over.

He left the rink and trudged through the snow back to the team's hotel. People passed him on the street and smiled at him and said, "Bonjour." He simply nodded. He was deep in thought.

He thought back on the season. How his wicked temper had caused people all kinds of grief. How his losing Turtles had been transformed into winning River Rats by a couple of teenagers who preached fair play and sportsmanship. How he'd been insanely jealous of the Mitchell kids. How he'd dumped a load of sand and gravel all over their new rink. How stupid was that? How he'd even become a common thief by stealing one of their hockey sticks. That was a minor crime. How he'd paid the Slugg Brothers and their cronies to beat up the Mitchells and all but kidnap the parents. Another crime. *How could I be so despicable?* he thought. *Surely my nephew—and the players I've coached—despise me. They looked to me for guidance, and what did I give them? Nothing.*

He kicked at a lump of hard-packed snow that lay in his path. "What a fool I've been," he muttered aloud. "What an absolute fool!"

An attractive young woman pulling a child on a sleigh walked toward him. He stepped aside, allowing her to pass.

"Bonjour, monsieur," she called out cheerily.

He gave her a sad smile. "Bonjour, madame."

Back at the rink, half a period was left to play. The coachless Terrors wandered around the ice, listless and leaderless.

The referee was about to drop the puck when Wally Wilson emerged from the Turtle Creek dressing room. He wore a large patch above his eye, but his eyes were as clear as his convictions.

He approached the game officials and the Mitchell brothers.

"Let's finish this tournament and this season with a bang," he suggested. "Let's show the fans ten minutes of good, clean hockey. It'll erase some of the shame we feel."

"Great idea," Max said, enthused. "Let's show them the kind of hockey that's truly representative of the North Country."

"It'll be a great way to end the season," Marty agreed.

And that's the way the tournament ended. The River Rats and the Terrors gave the fans who remained a wonderful display of peewee hockey at its finest. The kids on both teams finally had a chance to excel without being distracted by broken rules and overly aggressive play. While it lasted, the game became a showcase for swift skating, expert playmaking and hard shooting. And the goaltenders—one in particular—performed brilliantly. In the end, it was tiny Nicole Falzone who skated off with a 2–0 shutout and a deafening ovation ringing in her ears.

A red carpet was hastily spread along the ice. In two languages, the River Rats were named "Winners of the first peewee tournament in Quebec." As captain, Tim Robbins was the first of the River Rats to hoist the trophy high above his shoulders and skate around the ice with it. Then Nicole, the Stanowski twins and all the others had their turn. How bright-eyed and excited they were.

Squirt drew a gasp from the crowd when he took his turn. He forgot about the red carpet, stumbled over it and almost fell. The trophy popped from his hands and flew high in the air. But Nicole moved in smartly and caught it before it hit the ice. Another great save! And another great cheer rocked the building.

Nicole won more sustained applause when she was named top goalie of the tournament. Another ovation—not as prolonged, perhaps—greeted Chubby Morris when he was named first star in the final game for his winning goal.

Max and Marty were asked to take a bow as the winning coaches. The applause they received from the crowd was generous and was matched by the slapping of sticks on the ice and a noisy cheer from the River Rats.

The biggest ovation was reserved for Tim Robbins, who modestly accepted a gleaming silver trophy as tournament MVP.

Max and Marty looked on, their eyes moist.

"I've never felt so much pride," Max said. "Wait till we get back home. There'll be a celebration like we've never seen before. And these kids deserve it." He turned his head away and wiped a tear from his cheek. In the stands he saw Silas Stanowski beaming happily. His sons had contributed so much. Thank God they hadn't drowned in the farm pond. He watched as Silas put his arm around Miss Fallis and kissed her affectionately on the cheek.

Marty sniffled and reached for a handkerchief.

He blew his nose—hard.

"Hey, Max," Marty said, putting an arm around his brother. "Remember early in the season when Whizzer quit the team. And they asked us to coach. And we almost said no. Aren't you glad we didn't?"

Max took Marty's arm and squeezed it to his side.

"Best thing we ever did, Marty. What a pleasure it's been."

THE REST OF THE STORY

The River Rats returned home to a tumultuous reception. People met their train, and the team was promptly paraded down Main Street in open convertibles while confetti was tossed from high buildings—the highest being three stories.

Harry Mitchell arranged for a two-page spread on the team's triumph to appear in the *Review*, and the Mayor presented the players and coaches with wristwatches.

Silas Stanowski and Stella Fallis were married in June. Dino Falzone served as best man, and the twins spoke glowingly of their new stepmother at the reception. The couple honeymooned at Niagara Falls.

Nicole Falzone entered a short-story contest promoted by a popular kids' magazine and won first-prize money of 100 dollars. Her essay was entitled "No Girls Allowed."

Joe Stanowski, who never made an appearance in our story, spent time with his new friend Max over the summer. They shared their mutual interest in science projects. Joe was thrilled to earn a scholarship to Harvard University and left for Boston in September.

Whizzer Wilson left the area for a few months. He underwent psychiatric treatment in Montreal and learned how to manage his anger. He sent a note of congratulations to the Mitchell brothers and apologized for dumping sand and gravel on their rink. Inside the envelope was a crisp new 100-dollar bill. "For hockey expenses," the note explained. Whizzer said he was learning to speak French and that his brother Bill was looking after his sand and gravel business in his absence.

Most of the River Rats said they were looking forward to the next hockey season. Mr. Barnaby was certain Roddy would become an NHL player someday because "the coaches finally listened to him and put Roddy back on defence where he always belonged."

Mrs. Thomas gave Chubby's goalie pads to the Salvation Army. Chubby joined a band—the River Ramblers—organized by lead guitar player Danny Winters.

Max and Marty were invited to a farewell party for a man they truly admired—Judge Horace Gaul. Judge Gaul was appointed to the highest court in the land. At first, Marty was suspicious. He thought Judge Gaul's appointment was some kind of practical joke.

Other than that, nothing much happened in Indian River. It's a pretty quiet place.